"I'm not leaving you alone, Robyn. We're going to stick together from here on out."

Until when? Her memory had returned? And what if it didn't? Obviously Slade intended to protect her and hoped his efforts wouldn't be in vain.

She knew full well if she couldn't testify, then she was of no use to him.

"I'm sorry we had to escape another safe house," Slade said.

"It's not your fault." Her shivering was slowing down, and exhaustion pulled at her. She blinked, trying to stay awake. "I'm sorry I lost my memory."

"That's not your fault, either," Slade murmured.

Despite their dire circumstances, she found herself smiling.

They were both wet and cold, huddling together for warmth. This closeness she felt toward Slade wasn't anything more than two people depending on each other to stay alive.

No point in wasting time thinking about her handsome marshal. Her focus right now needed to be on regaining her memory.

Before whoever had attempted to kill her tried again.

Laura Scott has always loved romance and read faith-based books by Grace Livingston Hill in her teenage years. She's thrilled to have been given the opportunity to retire from thirty-eight years of nursing to become a full-time author. Laura has published over thirty books for Love Inspired Suspense. She has two adult children and lives in Milwaukee, Wisconsin, with her husband of thirty-five years. Please visit Laura at laurascottbooks.com, as she loves to hear from her readers.

Books by Laura Scott

Love Inspired Suspense

Justice Seekers

Soldier's Christmas Secrets
Guarded by the Soldier
Wyoming Mountain Escape
Hiding His Holiday Witness

Callahan Confidential

Shielding His Christmas Witness
The Only Witness
Christmas Amnesia
Shattered Lullaby
Primary Suspect
Protecting His Secret Son

Alaska K-9 Unit

Tracking Stolen Secrets

Visit the Author Profile page at Harlequin.com for more titles.

HIDING HIS HOLIDAY WITNESS

LAURA SCOTT

LOVE INSPIRED SUSPENSE
INSPIRATIONAL ROMANCE

LOVE INSPIRED® SUSPENSE
INSPIRATIONAL ROMANCE

ISBN-13: 978-1-335-72270-6

Recycling programs
for this product may
not exist in your area.

Hiding His Holiday Witness

This edition published by arrangement with Harlequin Books S.A.

For questions and comments about the quality of this book, please contact us at CustomerService@Harlequin.com.

Love Inspired
22 Adelaide St. West, 40th Floor
Toronto, Ontario M5H 4E3, Canada
www.Harlequin.com

Printed in U.S.A.

And so it was, that, while they were there, the days were accomplished that she should be delivered. And she brought forth her firstborn son, and wrapped him in swaddling clothes, and laid him in a manger; because there was no room for them in the inn.

—*Luke* 2:6-7

This book is dedicated to my friend Lori Handeland.
I'm so happy to have you in my life!

ONE

Robyn Lowry couldn't sleep, frowning when she heard a scraping noise against the side of the safe house. An unusual sound and something she hadn't heard in the past week. She froze, then quickly slid from the bed. Pulling a dark sweatshirt over her head, she grabbed her jeans and shrugged into them. After stuffing her feet into navy blue running shoes, she silently eased the basic cell phone provided by the US Marshals off its charger.

Marshal Craig Wainwright should be sitting in the main living area of the house. Unless he'd gone outside for some reason, like to make rounds? Was that what she'd heard? She didn't know Marshal Craig very well; Marshal Slade Brooks covered the day shifts, leaving nights for others.

Only she didn't think the marshal was outside. He wouldn't leave her alone without a really good reason. Every one of her instincts was flashing red alert.

Something was wrong.

Flattening herself against the wall, she peered through the bedroom window. She didn't see anything but darkness, the moon obliterated by clouds and only a glimpse of the snowcapped Rocky Mountains off in the distance.

Her imagination? After what she'd been through, she wasn't about to ignore her gut. And right now, everything inside was screaming at her to get out.

Abandoning the window, she tiptoed through the dark house, making her way toward the living area. There was no sign of Craig. She swiftly crossed to the front door. The scraping sound had come from the back of the house, and the safe house was located on a dead-end road.

The house across the street was supposedly empty, the owners away on a three-week cruise over the Christmas holidays.

Her pulse quickened. By the time she called for help, the bad guy would be inside. There was no time to waste. Looking through the front-door window, her gaze scoured the front yard. It was bare of anything but frost-tipped grass and one tall aspen tree, not large enough for anyone to hide behind.

Even her.

Okay, then. She turned the knob on the front door. Why was it unlocked?

She heard glass shattering.

Someone was breaking in!

Robyn flew across the yard, her sneakers making indentations in the frosted grass. She sprinted toward the vehicle parked on the road, hoping, praying she'd find Craig out here for some reason. But as she stared at the windshield, there wasn't anyone behind the wheel.

Was she mistaken? Could the broken glass have come from the federal marshal? But if so, why?

She wrenched the car door open, praying the keys were in the ignition.

They weren't.

No time! She couldn't waste any more time!

In a low crouch, Robyn eased alongside the vehicle, then stopped abruptly when she saw a small dark puddle forming beneath the trunk of the car.

Blood.

She stared, her brain unwilling to believe. But there was no mistake. *Drip. Drip. Drip.* No, no, it couldn't be—in her mind she envisioned the body of the dead marshal in the trunk. Her stomach heaved, but there was no time to be sick. She touched the car. Maybe he was still alive and she could help him.

She heard a door slam. Her pursuer must have left the house.

Move, she told herself. *Go!* She ran across the street to the vacant house as fast as her feet could carry her, imagining she was back in college running track and determined to win.

Or, in this case, stay alive.

The back of the house offered little protection. Fearing her footprints were leaving a trail that a blind man could follow on the stiff grass, she tried to choose her path carefully. December temperatures had been milder than normal, but it was still chilly at this hour of the morning. When she reached the next street, she instinctively veered to the left. She paused in the shadows of a large oak, searching for her phone when she heard the muffled thudding of footsteps against asphalt.

No! He was following her!

Panic gripped her by the throat. Whoever the guy was, he'd already harmed a federal agent. And there was no doubt she was the ultimate target.

A dead witness couldn't testify against the mighty Elan Gifford, gunrunner and general mobster extraordinaire.

Putting on a burst of speed, she darted across the road, searching for cover. This section of the small town of Timnath, Colorado, didn't offer much in the way of protection. Which, ironically, had been one of the reasons the federal marshals had chosen the location.

Close enough to get to Denver for the trial.

Far enough out of Denver to be safe.

Only she wasn't safe. Not anymore. Maybe never again.

Robyn needed to find a hiding spot so she could call Slade Brooks, the US deputy marshal she trusted the most. She sent up a silent prayer of thanks that Slade wasn't injured or, worse, dead in the trunk of a car, and asked God to watch over Marshal Craig.

She ran, her mind frantic. Where should she go?

The church!

She jutted around another corner and sprinted toward the church that was about a mile off in the distance.

She'd run farther for less.

Keeping to the shadows as much as possible, Robyn made her way in a zigzag pattern to the building. It would be locked in the middle of the night, but the quaint structure called to her in a way she couldn't explain.

Ten minutes later, she reached her destination. She didn't stop until she was hidden in the shadows alongside the church wall.

For long minutes she could only hear her ragged breathing and the thundering beat of her heart. She struggled to calm herself, needing to listen closely in order to determine if the bad guy had managed to keep up with her.

Thankful for the dark clothing she wore, and the

lack of snow, she crouched low and swept a keen eye over the area from which she'd come.

Just as she was about to pull out her phone to call Slade, she saw her follower. A man dressed in black lightly jogging across the road and taking cover behind a tree.

The same tree she'd hidden behind minutes earlier.

A panicked scream clawed up her throat. She melted back against the building, moving with excruciating slowness toward the rear of the church while keeping her gaze locked on the tree and the shadow of the man in black.

He hadn't moved in the time it took her to reach the church corner. Was he standing there because he wasn't sure where she'd gone? Maybe God had helped cover her footprints.

Then he crept out from behind the tree, turning his head from side to side as if looking for her.

The clouds moved away from the moon, and a shaft of moonlight illuminated his pale profile.

Shock sent a horrified stillness through her. No, it couldn't be. She'd cared for him.

Betrayal cut like a knife. The sick certainty sank deep into her bones.

How had he found her?

She had no answer, but the need to get somewhere safe intensified.

Because if he'd been sent by Gifford's men, she knew he wouldn't stop until she was dead.

She eased around the corner, scanning the area behind the church for somewhere to hide. The back door of the parish caught her eye, and she hurried over to check the door just in case. Holding her breath, she opened the screen door first, then tried the inside door handle.

It was unlocked!

Sending up a quick prayer of thanks to God for providing this chance to escape, she pushed the door open and crept inside. The darkness swallowed her, but she didn't mind.

Being here felt safe from the hunter outside.

She locked the door and eased farther into the back of the church. She wasn't familiar with this section of the building, behind the pulpit. She'd attended church twice and always sat in the back row. When she was far enough from the rear door, she pulled out her phone and called the only number she had listed in the device.

Slade's number.

The phone rang three times before his sleepy voice answered, "Robyn? Something wrong?"

"Yes." The sound of his low, husky voice brought an overwhelming sense of relief, but she still couldn't relax. Her pursuer was out there, and just as she was about to tell Slade what was wrong, she heard the knob to the back door rattle, as if someone was trying it to see if it would open.

She froze. She couldn't leave. He might see her. Her eyes lit on another door, and she pulled it open, careful not to make any noise. Just as she was about to take a step down into the building's basement, her toe caught on the lip of a tread.

Thrust off balance, she dropped the phone while trying to grab something for support. Her fingers caught the edge of the doorjamb, then slipped away as she slid down the stairs.

Pain ricocheted through her brain, and then there was nothing but darkness.

"Robyn? Robyn!" Slade jackknifed out of bed, reaching for his clothes. There had been loud thumping noises through the phone, but then nothing but silence.

He grabbed his gun and his badge, then shoved his feet into his shoes. He hit the front door of the rental house like a linebacker going for a quarterback. As he ran to the car, he tried to reach Craig Wainwright, the federal marshal on graveyard duty at Robyn's safe house.

The call went straight to voice mail.

It was a bad sign. Craig was a good marshal; he should answer his phone. Where was he? And where was Robyn? Slade hit the gas, sending the car careening out of the driveway and onto the street.

For security reasons, his rental house was on the other side of the small town of Timnath. It was the main place they slept when they weren't on duty. Earlier that day, Tyler Ryerson had gone back to Denver with the news his wife was about to deliver their baby, so Slade was on his own. Thankfully he wasn't too far from Robyn's safe house.

There was no traffic on the streets at two in the morning. A good thing, since he drove straight down the middle of the road, his gaze sweeping the area for a sign that Gifford's men had found the safe house.

It was impossible to imagine how they had accomplished such a feat. No one had access to the federal marshals' safe house location.

Their job was to keep federal witnesses alive.

If something bad happened to Robyn... He couldn't finish the thought.

She had to be okay. She just had to be!

He called his boss, James Crane, using the hands-free function as he drove. "Robyn Lowry's safe house has been breached. I can't reach Craig and need backup. Tyler Ryerson is still in Denver."

"I'll send the locals there immediately."

Slade disconnected the call, having reached the safe house in record time. Craig's vehicle was parked on the street, but he barely gave it a second glance, his gaze focused on the safe house. There were no lights on that he could see. But as he jumped out from behind the wheel and headed up toward the front door, he sucked in a harsh breath when he saw it was hanging open.

Holding his weapon in two hands, he swiftly and silently entered the house.

The main living space was clear, no one hiding beneath the table or in the closet. He made his way down to the bathroom, which was also empty, then to the bedrooms.

They were empty. But in the bedroom that Robyn was clearly living in, there was a broken window.

He made quick work of clearing the rest of the house. Returning outside to Craig's vehicle, he found the driver's-side door wasn't closed all the way. Careful not to disturb any fingerprints, he opened the door and looked inside.

Nothing. Where was Craig Wainwright?

On a whim, he hit the switch for the trunk and hurried around back.

Craig's body was stuffed in the trunk, a bullet hole in his temple.

He stumbled back from the horrific scene, his mind whirling. There was no time to grieve for his fellow marshal. Robyn was in deep trouble.

The urge to begin searching the area was strong. Where in the world was his backup?

Moving away from the vehicle, he searched the ground for footprints. He found what looked to be a small footprint in the frozen grass, likely from a running shoe heading away from the safe house and toward the vacant house across the street.

Red and blue lights lit up the sky, and he turned, relieved the locals had arrived. He quickly brought them up to speed on what had happened. It went against the grain to include them in a federal case, but he didn't have a choice.

Robyn needed to be found and kept safe.

"Marshal Brooks? I'm Officer Ted Michaels, and this is Officer Wendy Allen." Michaels got a glimpse of Craig's body. "Who is that?"

"Federal Marshal Craig Wainwright. He's been murdered, and my witness, Robyn Lowry, is in extreme danger." He flashed his five-point marshal badge. "I need you to put out a BOLO for Robyn Lowry, with instructions to keep her safe from harm. She's roughly five-five, weighs 125 pounds and has long, straight blond hair and is likely wearing dark clothing. She's unarmed and in danger, from the person who shot Marshal Wainwright, understand?"

"Got it." Officer Wendy Allen reached for her radio to relay the message.

"Spread out and search for the woman while keeping an eye out for the shooter, who we know is armed and dangerous." Slade gestured in the direction the footprints pointed. "I'm going that way to the south. I need each of you to head north and east. There's nothing to the west except the Poudre River."

"Are you sure she's alone? Maybe the guy who shot your cop has her," Officer Michaels suggested.

"Anything is possible, but I'm hoping he hasn't caught my witness yet. Let's cover the area on foot, see if we can find anything." He swallowed a flash of irritation at the way they were wasting time. "Take my phone number and call if you find anything."

He rattled it off and was impressed that Wendy was able to capture the numbers, punching them into her phone and then hitting the talk button to make sure the call went through.

"Thanks." Slade turned and headed out at a light jog. He knew Robyn was a runner and felt certain she would have done a good job in putting distance between herself and the shooter. Especially if she'd gotten a head start.

They'd run together a few times, and she'd easily kept pace with him. He felt certain that she could beat him in a race if needed.

Raking his gaze over the area, he tried to see it through her eyes. She'd be looking for a place to hide and call for help.

He caught the occasional disturbance on the

ground—flattened grass, a broken twig of a bush—but knew that there was a chance that they'd been caused by someone or something else.

Yet his gut told him he was on Robyn's trail.

His chest squeezed painfully at the thought of losing her. Not just losing Gifford's trial without their key witness, but losing *her*. Despite his attempt to view Robyn only as his most recent case, it had been difficult to ignore the underlying attraction that simmered between them.

At least on his part. He wasn't at all convinced she felt the same way. Which was for the better in the long run. He'd already lost one woman he'd loved; he wasn't ready to replace her.

Come on, Robyn, where are you?

There was no sign of her, or anyone else, for that matter. Slade wanted to believe the shooter was long gone but kept his weapon in his hand just in case.

Did Robyn know about Craig's murder? She was smart—she might have figured out something was wrong when he'd left her alone.

He stared at their surroundings, feeling helpless. Was it possible she'd gone to one of the residences on the street for help? He didn't think so, but then again, he'd been wrong before.

Had been wrong when he'd followed his instincts with a previous witness, six months ago.

His witness, Brett Thompson, had died because of him.

Slade pulled out his cell phone and tried calling Robyn again. As before, the phone went unanswered. He held on to the faint hope that the phone wasn't damaged or turned off, as the call didn't go straight to voice mail.

Yet in the darkest corner of his mind, he understood Robyn couldn't answer the phone if she was dead.

No. *No!* He refused to think that way. He'd been raised to believe in God, but since Brett's murder, and almost losing Chelsey, the guy's fiancée, on the heels of Marisa's death, he'd found it impossible to pray.

As soon as the thought entered his mind, he saw the church steeple rising out from behind the residences lining the street.

The church? Robyn had insisted on attending church services twice in the past week, which in his opinion had been two times too many. Not so much because it was wrong to attend church, but establishing any sort of routine while hiding in plain sight wasn't smart.

Would she go there now? In the middle of the night while running from danger? He picked up his pace, knowing the church was the only clue he had to go on.

Keeping a wary eye out for the shooter, he made his way up to the building. The front door with its beautiful stained-glass window faced the road, welcoming all to enter.

The front of the church was too open for anyone to go in this way without being seen, but he decided to check the door just in case. No surprise to find it locked.

Slade moved around the building, choosing the side covered in shadows. He could imagine Robyn doing the same thing, searching for a hiding spot in the sanctuary.

The back door? Maybe. He inched closer, and his heart nearly stopped in his chest when he noticed the screen door was slightly ajar.

He pulled it open and tried the door handle. The inside door was locked. His shoulders slumped with defeat. He'd felt certain he was on the right path.

Turning away, he thought about the phone. He hit the redial button and listened intently.

A faint ringing could be heard from somewhere inside.

Yes! He glanced around, then slammed into the door with his shoulder. Once, twice, a third time until the wood frame gave way.

Inside, he used the flashlight app, sweeping his phone over the back of the church. Robyn's phone was on the floor near a stairwell leading down into what looked to be a basement.

The beam of his light picked up Robyn's form, lying on the ground at the bottom of the stairs. He headed down, his palms damp with sweat as he checked for a pulse.

She moaned and shifted. Feeling the beat of her heart beneath his fingertips brought a wave of relief.

"Robyn? Can you hear me? It's okay, you're safe now." He gently felt along the back of her head. There was a lump, but no evidence of blood.

Was that a good thing? He wasn't sure.

"Robyn? Can you hear me?"

Her beautiful desert-brown eyes blinked and focused on his face. "Where am I?"

"In the church basement. You fell down the stairs. Where does it hurt?"

"My head." She winced and put a hand up to gently touch the bump. Then she looked at him in confusion. "Why am I here? Who are you?"

He froze. "You don't remember me?"

"Should I?" She struggled to sit up, but he put a hand on her shoulder to hold her still.

"My name is Slade Brooks. I'm one of the US deputy marshals assigned to protect you."

The blank expression in her eyes made him feel sick. "Why do I need protection?"

He stared at her, his thoughts whirling. "You're a key witness in the Elan Gifford trial, remember?"

"Me?" The confusion intensified. "What's my name?"

"Robyn Lowry."

There was no hint of recognition in her gaze. Only confusion and fear.

Slade swallowed hard. Their key witness didn't know who she was or why she was here.

Gifford's trial was scheduled to start in five days.

How could Robyn testify without her memory?

TWO

Her name was Robyn? The throbbing pain made it difficult to concentrate.

"What else hurts, Robyn? Besides your head?" The man hovering over her had jet-black hair and chiseled features. He spoke to her as if they knew each other, but for some reason she couldn't place him.

Although there was something way in the back of her mind that made him seem familiar.

She flexed her arms and legs. "Nothing, really." It wasn't entirely true. There were aches and pains throughout her body, but from what she could tell, no broken bones. "Help me up."

"No, please stay where you are. I'll call for an ambulance. You could have a neck or back injury to go along with the bump on your head. You need to be checked out at the hospital."

"I'm fine," she insisted, but of course he didn't listen. He was on the phone talking to a cop, letting him know she was okay but needed an ambulance sent to the church.

She was in a church? Why? How had she gotten here?

"The ambulance will be here shortly," the dark-haired man said, kneeling beside her.

She frowned trying to remember what he'd said earlier. "I'm sorry, what was your name again?"

There was a long pause before he said, "I'm US Deputy Marshal Slade Brooks. You're a witness scheduled to testify in a trial. Does the name Elan Gifford mean anything to you?"

"No." His expression turned grim, and she sensed she was disappointing him. She put a hand up to her head. "I'm sure once my head stops hurting, I'll be able to remember."

Slade nodded. "Try to relax. You're safe now."

Safe. A shiver rippled over her. There was no denying she felt safe with Slade beside her, but how had she ended up here? Lying on the floor in a church basement?

A stab of fear hit hard. Deep down, she felt as if she needed to move. To run.

"We should get out of here," she whispered.

Slade leaned forward, his keen gaze boring into hers. "Why? Do you remember something?"

"No." The more she tried to remember, the more her head hurt. She closed her eyes and pressed a hand to her stomach, praying she wouldn't throw up. "But I feel like we need to go someplace safe."

"We will, after we get you checked out at the hospital." Slade smoothed her hair from her face. "You can trust me to keep you safe, Robyn."

"Robyn with an *i* or a *y*?"

He looked surprised by her question. "Which way do you like better?"

"Robyn with a *y*, but that doesn't mean my parents spelled it that way."

"They did," he said softly, a small smile brightening his features. "You're Robyn with a *y*, and your last name is Lowry."

The name sounded a little familiar. Panic threatened to overwhelm her, and she tried to do as Slade suggested, relax and rest, providing time for her short-circuited brain cells to return to normal.

The wail of sirens made her clench with the urge to run. Which was the wrong answer, wasn't it? Shouldn't she head toward those in authority rather than running away?

Slade started to rise, but she grabbed his hand. "Don't leave me."

He glanced down at her in surprise. "I won't. But the EMTs aren't going to know where we are. I need to show them the way inside."

Swallowing hard, she released him. "Okay, but hurry."

"Don't worry. I'll get you the care you need."

Alone on the basement floor, there was no way to rest or relax. Every muscle in her body was tense as she waited for Slade to return.

He'd left his phone flashlight on for her. The thoughtful gesture made her wonder about Slade Brooks. How long had she known him? Were they friendly?

More than friendly?

Stupid thought. She wasn't swayed by physical attraction, although Slade certainly had that in spades, but his kind and caring disposition was endearing.

What had he said? She was a witness?

The pain in her head intensified when she thought about the name he'd mentioned, Elan Gifford.

There was something hazy in the back of her mind, but it was as elusive as catching snowflakes with your fingers.

Why couldn't she remember?

The two EMTs came clattering down the basement stairs. She suffered through their poking and prodding, answering their questions to the best of her ability.

"She didn't remember her name, or mine for that matter," Slade informed them. "And we've been together for the past week."

"Amnesia?" The EMT to her right sounded concerned.

"I'm sure my memory will clear up when my

headache eases off a bit." Robyn wasn't at all convinced that would happen, but it sounded good. And right now, she needed to believe it to be true.

"Pupils are equal and reactive to light," the paramedic to her left said. "They'll need to do a CT scan of her head to make sure she doesn't have an intracranial bleed."

"I'm going with you," Slade said as they lifted her onto the gurney and strapped her down. Being unable to move her arms and legs was unnerving.

"You can't," the EMT to her right protested.

Slade flashed his badge. "Try to stop me."

The two EMTs glanced at each other and shrugged. With efficient movements, they collapsed the gurney and carried her up the stairs to the main level.

The bright red flashing lights of the ambulance added to her fierce pain. She winced and closed her eyes, again willing herself not to throw up.

She heard Slade saying something to the police officers, then he joined her in the back of the ambulance. She was relieved to have him close at hand. For one thing, he knew who she was, more than she did. And with nothing but Swiss cheese in her brain, she needed the stability of his presence.

She believed Slade would keep her safe.

* * *

Slade tried not to panic over Robyn's amnesia as they rode to the closest hospital, which happened to be located in Fort Collins, Colorado.

Should he tell his boss? Or wait to see if her memory returned? He knew true amnesia was rare, but no way was Robyn faking this.

What would be her motive for doing such a thing? It wasn't as if the federal government was forcing her to testify.

She'd insisted on it. Had been the one to turn in everything she'd uncovered about Elan Gifford's gunrunning crimes to the authorities. First the money trail she'd discovered working as his store manager when the accounts hadn't added up correctly, and then the pictures of the guns themselves. The feds had asked the US Marshal services for help in protecting their witness, which was why he'd been sent to Colorado.

He wanted to be out working the case, finding out who had murdered his colleague Craig Wainwright. The guy had left a wife and a child behind. When he'd contacted his boss about Craig's death and finding Robyn, the man had agreed to send Slade's buddy Colt Nelson up from Wyoming to help, since Tyler Ryerson was still in Denver with his newborn son.

Slade trusted Colt and his other friend Tanner

with his life. Had worked the Brett Thompson case with them several months ago. Slade had tried to get Brett Thompson into the witness protection program, but the guy had wanted to wait until after his wedding. Only Brett had been shot and killed.

Losing another witness meant a career change was in his future. If anything happened to Robyn, he wouldn't blame his boss for firing him once this was over.

The ambulance pulled up in front of the emergency department, and two scrubs-clad figures came out to meet them. The woman with a name tag identifying her as a physician pushed him out of the way.

"I'm US Marshal Slade Brooks," he said, keeping pace alongside Robyn's gurney. "This woman is in my protective custody."

"Stay out of my way" was the doctor's response.

He swallowed his frustration, knowing they were focused on caring for Robyn's injuries. He stood off to the side as the medical team surrounded her. In what looked to be controlled chaos, they moved her from the ambulance gurney to a bed, connected her to monitors and used a stethoscope to listen to her heart, her lungs, her stomach.

Medical jargon flew between them as the team rattled off her vital signs and other key components of her care. Most he was able to follow, but not all of it. He noticed the doctor spent a lot of time asking Robyn questions she couldn't answer.

Oh, Robyn knew the president, vice president and other big events that had happened in the not-too-distant past, but she couldn't remember anything about herself, her name, her family, where she lived.

The expressions on the medical team's faces indicated they were concerned.

Which made him doubly so.

"Let's get her into the CT scanner ASAP while we wait for the neurosurgeon to get here." The female physician glanced at Slade for the first time since telling him to stay out of the way. "I assume you're going with her?"

"Yes." Her name tag identified her as Dr. Florian.

"Fine." Dr. Florian glanced at one of the nurses. "Call me when the scan has been completed."

"Will do." The nurse disconnected the monitor and pushed the bed away from the wall. Slade quickly took his place beside Robyn.

"You doing okay?" he asked as the nurse and an orderly pushed her down the hall.

"Yes." Robyn's voice was strained, and he felt certain she was anything but okay.

He wanted to reach out and take her hand, to reassure himself that she'd get through this. He winced thinking of Craig Wainwright's murder.

How Robyn had managed to escape the shooter was beyond comprehension.

But then, he'd already known she was brave and determined to do the right thing.

No matter what the cost.

The scan took longer than he anticipated, maybe because they checked her from head to toe, so it was a solid forty-five minutes until they were back in the emergency department.

The neurosurgeon arrived shortly thereafter, asking Robyn all the questions the previous doctor has asked. The minutes dragged by with agonizing slowness. He'd been hoping for answers, but it seemed like the doctors came and went without saying much of anything.

Finally, Dr. Florian returned. "Ms. Lowry?"

Robyn's eyes remained closed. Slade put his hand on her shoulder. "Robyn?"

She opened her eyes and looked confused for a moment before focusing her gaze on Dr. Florian. "Are you talking to me?"

"Yes, I wanted to let you know that you don't have any broken bones per the CT scan, but you do have a very small subdural hemorrhage. It's likely the source of your—uh, memory problems."

"What does that mean?" Slade asked with a frown. "Is she going to be all right?"

"The neurosurgeon would like you to stay for observation," she informed Robyn. "It's close to dawn now, so they'll keep you for at least twenty-four hours and do a follow-up CT scan tomorrow morning. If the bleed is unchanged, they'll likely discharge you home. The neurosurgeons feel that rest is the best way for your memory to return." Dr. Florian shifted her gaze to Slade. "I told them you'd be staying with her."

"I will, yes." Although his boss would insist on having another deputy cover the night shift. The thought of letting Robyn out of his sight didn't sit well.

Look what had happened last time.

Slade's phone rang, and he was relieved to see the call was from Colt. "Hey, how far out are you?"

"Hello to you, too," Colt drawled. "I hear you've got problems."

"Big ones," he admitted. "I could really use your help."

"I'm in Jackson but should be there in about seven hours, nine at the latest. Where should I meet up with you?"

"I'm at the Fort Collins Hospital. They're going to keep Robyn here overnight."

"I heard about Wainwright." Colt's tone was somber. "We need to find the guy who shot him."

"Yeah, we sure do, but we also need to keep Robyn safe." And that was the hard part, staying here and watching over her while others searched for clues.

"What does she remember about what happened?"

"Nothing, and that's the problem." Slade hadn't told his boss about Robyn's amnesia but knew he couldn't sit on this for long. If her memory didn't return…he didn't want to think about the fact that Gifford might get off scot-free. "I'll explain when you get here."

"Okay, see you in a bit." Colt clicked off the call.

Less than an hour later, Robyn was settled in a regular hospital room. The light bothered her eyes, so he lowered the shades and sat between her and the door.

The hours dragged by slowly, but Slade refused to leave Robyn alone even for a second. He was hungry, thirsty and would have stood on his head for a cup of coffee but didn't move from his post other than to use the restroom.

Eight hours later, Colt arrived. His fellow marshal had called ahead when he hit the city limits and brought burgers and fries from a fast-food joint.

"Thanks," Slade said gratefully. He glanced at Robyn, who had woken up when Colt entered the room. She seemed to be sleeping a lot—according to the nurse who came in periodically to check on her, that was a good thing. "Robyn, are you hungry?"

She grimaced and shook her head. "Not really. Although soup sounds good."

"I'll call the nurse. She'll get that for you." Slade reached for the call light, but Robyn already had it in her hand.

"I'm not helpless." She looked at Colt. "Am I supposed to know you, too?"

"Uh, I don't think so. I'm US Deputy Marshal Colt Nelson." He reached over to shake her hand, glancing curiously at Slade. "Nice to meet you."

Robyn offered a weak smile. "These aren't the best circumstances, though, are they?"

"No, ma'am," Colt agreed.

After Robyn's soup had been ordered, Slade filled Colt in on Robyn's escape from the safe house, her fall and resulting amnesia.

"Not good," Colt murmured.

"I know." He unwrapped his burger, then glanced at Robyn. "Will it bother you if we eat in here?" His stomach was growling like a bear in springtime, but Robyn's health had to take priority.

"Of course not, please eat. You've been here for hours." Robyn frowned. "Do I really need to stay here until tomorrow? It seems silly when there's nothing they're doing for me other than offering pain meds."

"Which you keep refusing," Slade pointed out with a frown. "It wouldn't hurt to take the edge off your headache."

"I don't like pain pills." The familiar stubborn jut of her chin was reassuring. Despite her memory issues, it seemed Robyn's basic personality remained intact.

Slade took a bite of his burger, trying not to wolf it down in record time.

"Boss called, wants to talk to me," Colt said when they'd finished their meal. Robyn had finished her soup, too, and she looked better, at least to Slade's inexpert eye. "I'll head over to the motel to discuss next steps, but will be back at around nine o'clock tonight to relieve you."

Slade rubbed the back of his neck. "Are you sure you're up to covering the night shift?"

"Yep." Colt's tone rang with confidence.

Slade stood and stretched, the inactivity wearing him down. "All right, but do me a favor, will you?"

Colt raised a brow. "Like?"

"Don't mention Robyn's amnesia to Crane." He flushed as Colt's eyebrows hiked up. "I know what you're thinking, but if her memory returns, everything will be fine."

"And if it doesn't?" Colt asked softly.

"Give me until tomorrow morning. That's when she's scheduled to have a repeat CT scan."

Colt sighed, ran a hand over his jaw and reluctantly nodded. "Yeah, okay. See you at nine."

The next two hours passed uneventfully, but then he heard a series of alarms going off in the hallway outside Robyn's room. The overhead speaker announced a code blue, and he felt certain that meant a medical emergency of some kind.

When the door to Robyn's room opened, he jumped to his feet, expecting to see the nurse who'd last checked in over two hours ago. Instead, Officer Ted Michaels stood there.

"What are you doing here?" Slade asked. Something about the guy was off.

In a flash, Michaels pulled his gun, pointing it at Slade. "Taking care of unfinished business."

Time stopped for a heartbeat as his brain instantly rolled through a variety of scenarios. Then several things happened at once. Robyn's call light began to ring, and the door behind Michaels opened.

The dual distractions worked in Slade's favor. He kicked upward, hitting Michaels's gun hand, pointing the weapon up toward the celling. A gunshot rang out, and the nurse who walked into the room screamed, but Slade was already on Michaels, trying to wrench the gun from his grip while slamming him up against the wall.

For long, terrible seconds they wrestled for the gun. Slade used his elbow to strike up at Michaels's face. The guy howled in pain and loosened his grip just enough for Slade to wrench the gun free.

"Call security. Hurry." He didn't look at the nurse, who'd finally stopped screaming; his focus centered on disarming Michaels and using the man's own cuffs to shackle him.

The nurse disappeared, and Slade glared at Michaels. "Who sent you?"

The cop's face went red, but he didn't answer. Slade wanted nothing more than to make him talk, but the need to get Robyn out of there was strong.

"Get dressed," he told Robyn. "Hurry. We need to go."

To her credit, Robyn didn't argue. She rolled off the mattress, scooped up her clothes and went into the bathroom. Less than a minute later, she emerged, her expression grim. By that time, he'd secured Michaels to the bed. He wasn't going anywhere.

He had Robyn out of the room just as two security officers were coming down the hall. "Hey, wait! You can't leave."

Slade pulled his weapon and held up his badge. "Can and will. Call the police. That guy in there was going to kill us."

Thankfully the security guards weren't armed. They gaped in surprise as Slade urged Robyn to the closest stairwell.

"We need to move fast," he whispered as they clambered down the stairs. "Where there's one dirty cop, there could be more."

"But why?" Robyn looked genuinely confused. "I don't understand."

"I don't, either." Slade didn't like this recent attempt—from a local cop, no less.

At this point, he had no idea whom they could trust.

THREE

A policeman had tried to kill us.

Robyn ignored her lingering headache, following Slade as they quickly took the stairs down to the main level of the hospital. Without stopping, he urged her through the lobby and outside into the late-afternoon light.

Slade kept one hand on her arm as he used his phone. "Colt? One of the local cops is dirty. He tried to kill us. I need you to pick us up ASAP."

A squad car was sitting in a no-parking zone. A chill rippled down her spine as she realized the cop upstairs had intended to shoot them both, and then what? Act as if he'd come in to find them already dead? Or set it up to look like a murder-suicide?

How could someone be so cold, so heartless?

Slade took her arm and pulled her toward the side of the building, away from the main road.

Sirens screeched, and she felt the same sense of panic she'd experienced earlier, the one that made her want to run. They needed to hide. But where? Nothing looked familiar.

Except for Slade.

"This way." Slade led the way through a parking lot. For a moment she had the foolish idea he was going to steal a car, but instead, he went to the farthest corner of the lot and crouched behind a large beige minivan with a soccer decal on the back window.

He tugged her down beside him.

"What are we doing?" she asked in a whisper.

"Waiting for Colt." Slade's expression was grim as he raked his gaze over the area. "Right now, he's the only guy I trust."

"Are you sure?" She didn't know Colt, didn't know anyone, really, but so far the only person who'd consistently helped her out of trouble was Slade.

"I'm sure. I've worked with him before." Slade glanced at her. "I trust him and one other marshal by the name of Tanner Wilcox. But no one else."

She shivered again, partially because of the chill in the December air. "What about your boss?" She'd heard him tell Colt not to let their boss know about her amnesia.

Slade shook his head, then lifted his phone. "Colt? How close are you?"

She heard the response even though the phone

wasn't on speaker. "I just passed the hospital—the place is crawling with cops."

Bitter fear lodged in her throat. What if those cops caught them? How would they know whom to trust?

"We're in the southeast corner of the parking lot. There's a rear entrance you can use. We're behind a beige minivan."

"Be there in a few."

The seconds stretched for what seemed like an eternity. Then she caught a glimpse of a black SUV coming toward them. Slade didn't move, not until the vehicle was close enough to recognize the driver.

"Ready?" Slade asked as Colt stopped the SUV.

"Yes." Together they stood and darted out from behind the van to the SUV. Slade opened the back passenger door and urged her inside. To her surprise, he followed and shut the door.

"Go," Slade ordered. Then he looked at her. "We need to crouch down behind the seats."

She didn't hesitate but wedged herself behind Colt's driver's seat. For long minutes no one spoke. She sensed Colt was getting them far away from the hospital parking lot before asking questions.

Maybe Slade was right about trusting Colt. He seemed willing to do whatever was necessary without arguing.

"You can probably get up now. We're outside the Fort Collins city limits," Colt drawled.

Slade unfolded himself and eased into the back seat. Then he offered his hand. She placed her own in his without hesitation, the warm physical connection calming her racing heart.

It wasn't easy to let go, but she forced herself to in order to fasten her seat belt.

"Where to?" Colt asked. "Another safe house, I assume?"

Slade let out a harsh sound. "Yes, but not one associated with the marshals. We need to stay off the grid."

"A local cop really tried to kill you?"

"Yes," she answered when Slade didn't. "He referred to us as unfinished business."

Colt let out a low whistle. "We need to call Crane."

"No." Slade's voice was firm. "Not until we're someplace safe."

"I assume you don't want to head to Denver." Colt peered at one of the road signs. "You want to follow the river toward Greeley? Or head south toward Boulder?"

"Boulder is an hour from here," she said. "But it's a much bigger city than Greeley."

Both men were silent for a long moment. Slade reached out to touch her forearm. "Robyn, how do you know that?"

She frowned. "I—I'm not sure. I just do. Why, is that wrong?"

"No, it's correct," Slade assured her. "But other than the questions you answered for the doctor, you haven't offered anything else from your memory."

"The distance between cities isn't exactly a memory, is it?" She put a hand up to touch the lump on the back of her head.

"It's a memory because you live in Denver," he explained.

"I do?" She had no idea why that fact surprised her. Maybe because they'd been in Timnath and then Fort Collins, and it made sense to her that she must have lived there.

Apparently not.

"Yes." Slade's smile was strained. "I guess we'll have to find another hospital for you so that you can get your follow-up CT scan."

She shuddered with distaste. "I don't think so."

His brow furrowed. "Robyn, head injuries can be serious."

"I know, but really, what was the hospital doing for me anyway?"

"The nurses were monitoring you and making sure you didn't get any worse."

"And I haven't. My headache is better than when I came in." Not by a lot, but it was tolerable. "No reason to risk getting a CT scan unless my condition gets worse."

"You're not a doctor or a nurse," Slade pointed out.

"Maybe not, but I'm the best one to decide how I'm feeling." She wondered what she did for a living and was about to ask when Colt interrupted.

"Robyn is right. After what happened back in Fort Collins, we can't risk taking her to another hospital unless her condition changes for the worse."

A muscle ticked at the corner of Slade's mouth, a sign of his pent-up anger and frustration.

Wait a minute, how did she know that?

She closed her eyes and relaxed, letting her thoughts drift like a sailboat on the ocean. She imagined seeing the waves, trying to capture the sound of them softly crashing onto the beach.

The pain in her head eased. She took a long, slow breath in and then let it out.

She tried to picture herself at a job. Did she sit in an office? Or work in some sort of store? The moment she tried to remember, the throbbing pain returned with a vengeance.

Helpless tears pricked her eyelids. What was wrong with her? Why couldn't she remember?

A cop had tried to kill them, and she couldn't even remember her name or what she did for a living.

"Robyn? Are you okay?"

Slade's low, husky voice was her undoing. He was being so kind, so gentle, yet she was letting him down.

They were in danger because of her. Because someone wanted to stop her from testifying against a man named Elan Gifford.

She had no idea how to fix it.

Slade watched helplessly as a tear slid from the corner of Robyn's eye, rolling down her cheek. She reached up and brushed it away.

"What's wrong? Is your headache worse?" He was scared to death that taking her out of the hospital would cause more harm than good.

"My head is fine." Her sharp tone caught him off guard. She grimaced and sighed. "I'm sorry. I just—you have no idea how frustrating it is not to remember anything."

"You don't have to apologize," Slade assured her. "This isn't your fault. We should have done a better job of protecting you."

"I'm still alive, so you're doing fine." A rueful smile tugged at the corner of her mouth. Crisis averted, at least for the moment. "I feel like I should ask you questions about my family, what I do for a living, the case, but—" she yawned and her eyelids drooped "—I'm so tired."

"Colt? Let's double back toward Greeley and make sure no one has followed us."

"Sure. I've been watching for a tail," Colt said. For a moment their gazes held via the rearview mirror. It wasn't that long ago that they'd thought they'd escaped without a tail, only to be proven wrong.

"Can you find us a motel that accepts cash?" Slade felt certain that rest was the best medicine for Robyn's amnesia.

And if it wasn't, well, he'd have to find another way. Letting Gifford walk wasn't an option.

"I have a better idea." Colt flashed a grin. "I can get us a small house for half the price."

He frowned. "You mean like through a vacation rental type of service? We can't leave a paper trail."

"Take my phone, see if you can find something close by."

"There's a house on the river in Greeley. It's private so it should work." Slade swallowed hard, not loving the river idea. Marisa had almost drowned during a river-rafting trip. Thankfully, he'd been able to pull her out of the water in time. Only to lose her a few months later, to an aggressive form of leukemia.

Since then, he'd remained focused on his career.

He glanced at Robyn, who was resting with her eyes closed, her head propped against the door. She was beautiful in a way that made his heart ache for something he didn't dare long for. He reminded himself that she was his witness, and that after she testified, he wouldn't see her again.

Based on the way Elan Gifford had at least one cop on his payroll, she was looking at the distinct possibility of being placed in witness protection.

And regardless of whether or not he was assigned as her handler, a relationship between them would be impossible.

A fact he'd do well to remember.

The sun was dipping down behind the horizon by the time Colt pulled up in front of their new safe house. It was a small, rather run-down place, but it was nice in that there weren't other homes nearby and the back of the house butted up against a small bluff overlooking the river.

"Robyn?" He touched her shoulder. "Can you walk or should I carry you?"

Her eyes rapidly opened at the suggestion. "Don't be silly. I can walk."

"Lean on me," he suggested, offering his arm. It wasn't at all silly from his perspective, but Robyn was independent.

Another part of her personality that hadn't been lost amid her amnesia. He'd been encouraged by her familiarity with Colorado and hoped it was a sign that her memory was coming back.

The ranch house was a bit dusty. He helped Robyn inside, moving through the living space to the bedrooms in the back, a similar layout to the house in Timnath. He glanced at Robyn to see if she noticed, but there was no recognition in her light brown eyes.

"I'm going to rest for a while." She headed straight toward the bed.

"Good plan." He double-checked that the bedroom windows were locked and lowered the blinds for her before leaving the room.

He joined Colt in the living room. "Boss left a message on my phone, wants to know what's up with the cuffed cop in Robyn's hospital room." Colt's expression was grim. "He's not happy we've been ignoring his calls."

"Yeah, well I'm not happy we were almost shot by a cop." Slade tempered his frustration. This mess was hardly Colt's fault. He'd just showed up in time to help him get Robyn to safety.

Was it possible God was watching over him? He wasn't convinced.

"You want me to call him?" Colt persisted. "He's not going to take no for an answer."

"I'll call him." Slade didn't like it, because cell phones could be traced. But he had to call Crane at least once, to let their boss know they were staying off the grid.

Until Robyn regained her memory, or until the trial. Whichever came first.

The sick feeling in his gut intensified, but for now all he could do was convince Robyn to rest and hopefully heal. The alternative was unthinkable. Gifford's dealing arms was bad, but killing a US deputy marshal was far worse. "Watch over Robyn for me. I'll be outside for a few minutes."

"Got it."

He glanced over his shoulder toward the bedroom door that he'd left open, not to violate her privacy but to hear her if she cried out in pain.

Or remembered something.

Outside, he turned his cell phone back on and winced when he saw he had the same message from his boss that Colt had. The level of anger in his boss's tone came through loud and clear.

"Where have you been!" Crane's voice boomed into his ear.

"I'm sorry, but my first responsibility is to keep the witness safe. Robyn's location has been compromised twice now in less than twenty-four hours."

The reminder of the US Marshal mission calmed Crane's tone a decibel. "Are you absolutely sure that cop was dirty? He's claiming you went nuts and attacked him, grabbing his gun and then cuffing him."

It hurt that his boss questioned his ethics, but then again, Slade had lost a witness six months ago. "Robyn was there during the interaction and will corroborate my story." It was ironic that she was able to remember that crime and not the one that she'd been placed in protection for in the first place. "He said he was there to take care of unfinished business."

His boss muttered something he couldn't hear. "Nelson is with you, I take it?"

"Yes, sir." Slade hesitated, then added, "We're planning to stay off the grid for a while. At least until we can figure out how Robyn's location keeps being found."

"Well, it's not as if being taken to the hospital was a secret," Crane said testily. "Anyone listening to the cop radio frequency knew that."

"Doesn't explain Craig's murder, though." Slade's tone was sharp. "Craig was a good marshal. He didn't deserve to be shot and shoved into the trunk."

"No, he didn't." The anger seemed to have faded from his boss's tone. Normally the most dangerous part of the job was issuing arrest warrants to known federal offenders. Those types of criminals tended to shoot first and ask questions later.

But this? Slade didn't like what was going on here at all.

Should he come clean about Robyn's amnesia? At some point, it occurred to him that if the word got out about her amnesia, the bad guys might stop coming after her.

Then again, maybe not. After all, there was the

possibility that the trial might be postponed until her memory returned.

If her memory returned.

"Brooks? You still there?" his boss asked irritably.

His exhaustion was getting to him. "Yes, I'm here. Listen, we have Robyn in a safe place. Don't ask me where. I'm not going to tell anyone. I'll be in touch in a couple of days."

"Every day," his boss snapped. "You can't go that far off the grid. I need to know you and Nelson are alive and kicking, understand?"

"Yes, sir. I'll call you tomorrow." Slade disconnected from the call and shut off his phone.

He stood for a moment, watching the last remnants of sunlight dip behind the horizon. For the first time since seeing Robyn lying at the bottom of the stairs, he felt as if they were finally safe.

It helped knowing Colt was here with him. If they could get Tanner to join them, the original three musketeers, then he'd be one hundred percent confident that they could handle anything that came their way.

He went inside and worked with Colt to perform a thorough examination of the property.

"There's no basement," he noted. "But unlike a motel, there is a back door."

"Yeah. And I like the way the backyard leads

to the bluff overlooking the river," Colt agreed. "This place should work fine for a couple of days."

Slade sincerely hoped so. As long as they weren't followed, and no one had tracked the brief call to his boss, they should be okay.

"Do we need to worry about any impending storms?" he asked.

Colt shook his head. "Not yet. The East Coast has been hit, but for some reason, we're still having mild temperatures here."

Slade would gladly take it. Escaping bad guys in a blizzard would be difficult. "We'd better get some sleep." He looked at Colt. "You want to take the first five hours or the second?"

"The first. No offense, buddy, but you look beat."

"Okay. Thanks." Slade made his way to the bedroom across from Robyn's.

He'd felt certain the events of the early-morning hours would replay over and over in his mind, but surprisingly, he slept. Until Colt shook him awake.

"My turn?" he asked groggily.

"There's a squad coming down the road. We need to get out of here."

A squad? He wasn't going to risk the fact that it might be nothing more than a coincidence.

He rolled out of bed and headed across the hall to Robyn's room. She'd fallen asleep fully dressed, which made for a quick escape.

"Robyn, we need to go."

Her eyes flew open, and she looked scared. Yet she didn't protest, simply got out of bed, put her shoes on and followed him out into the hall.

Colt quickly joined him. "There are two cops and it looks like they're splitting up, one likely coming around back. We need to beat him."

Two cops, circling the house. He urged Robyn to the back door and eased it open.

"Go," Colt urged. "I'll provide cover."

He didn't want to leave his buddy behind, but Robyn's safety had to come first. "You better join us ASAP," he murmured, then quickly stepped outside.

He took Robyn's hand and began to run. From somewhere behind him, he heard a shout. "Police! Stop or I'll shoot!"

Slade didn't stop and neither did Robyn. He heard the sound of gunfire as they reached the ridge. Without hesitation, he urged Robyn over the side, and they slid down toward the dark turbulent river.

Freezing-cold water surrounded him, stealing his breath. Slade tried not to panic as the swift current tugged and pulled at him.

And where was Robyn? Keeping his head above water was a challenge as he scoured the area for her.

Tight fear squeezed his chest, and flashbacks

to the near miss with Marisa threatened to overwhelm him. What if he'd rescued his key witness from a gunman only to lose her to the icy, roaring river?

FOUR

Robyn thrashed helplessly in the river current, her body numb from twin assaults of shock and the ice-cold water. Her awkward movements told her she wasn't the strongest swimmer on the planet, yet she hadn't drowned yet.

Although it was close as she was pulled beneath the water several times, only to resurface coughing out mouthfuls of river water.

Oddly enough, the cold water seemed to ease the pounding in her head. If the current wasn't so strong, she'd float on her back, resting most of her head in the soothing, cold water.

But floating along on her back wasn't an option.

As if on cue, the river sucked her under once again. She did her best to use her arms to return to the surface.

Gasping for air, she managed to keep her head above the water for several minutes and strained to listen. She'd heard two gunshots moments before Slade had gently pushed her over the ridge, but now there was only the rushing sound of water.

Did that mean they were safe? She had no idea.

And where was Slade?

Her heart pounded in fear as she tried to find him. The thought of being in the river all alone was horrifying, more so because she couldn't even remember her own name.

Slade! She needed to find Slade. She tried to turn in a circle, but the river was moving too fast for her to take more than a quick sweeping glance around to look for him.

It wasn't just that the river water pulled her along regardless of where she wanted to go; there were other dangers to watch out for. Her hip scraped painfully against a jutting rock, and a tree branch sticking out of the water nearly poked her in the eye.

She felt as if she were on some awful roller coaster without a safety belt.

Enough. She couldn't let the river win. Deep down, she knew she couldn't stay in the water for much longer without risking a severe case of hypothermia, despite the blessed lack of pain in her head. With renewed determination, Robyn angled toward the shore.

Her fingertips brushed against more rocks, only this time, she realized the shoreline was closer. Maybe even close enough that she could touch bottom.

The current was weaker now, as if this portion of the river was calmer than where she and Slade had gone in. Kicking her feet, she saw the shore grow closer. She kept going until she felt the river bottom against her soles.

The shore was just a few feet away!

But the river wouldn't let her go. She reached out but missed her attempt to grab a low-hanging tree branch. Frustrated, she gave another hard kick, angling even closer to the edge of the river.

There! Up ahead was another large tree branch hanging over the water. With a herculean effort, she reached up and snagged the branch. She clung to it for several long moments as the river tried to suck her back into its murky depths.

No. She wasn't going to let go. Taking a deep breath, she used every last bit of strength she possessed to pull herself up and out of the water.

Her feet found the ground, and she emerged from the river to sprawl on the grassy embankment.

For a moment all she could do was breathe heavily, shivering in the night. The December temperature was cool anyway, but being submerged in the river made it ten times worse.

"Slade?" Her voice was barely a croak. She

pushed her hair from her eyes and squinted through the darkness.

Where was he?

"Slade!" Panic clawed up her throat, threatening to strangle her.

She didn't know who she was or who was after her. She couldn't do this alone.

"Robyn!" The sound of her name made her want to weep with relief.

A splash caught her eye, and she saw a dark shadow getting out of the water about twenty yards from where she lay. Robyn told herself to get up and move, but her limbs were clumsy and heavy.

She turned onto her side and rested her head in the crook of her elbow. Maybe she'd just take a nap.

"Robyn." The voice was closer now, but she was too tired to respond. "Robyn, I'm so glad I found you. Stay with me. We need to get warm."

Warm? She frowned. She wasn't cold.

"Robyn? Talk to me." The voice was demanding now.

"Why?" She knew she sounded cranky. Reluctantly, she pushed herself upright. Strong arms pulled her close, and she was surprised to feel warmth radiating from him.

From Slade.

"Let's get into the cover of some brush, okay?"

Slade's voice was near her ear. "We want to stay hidden from view."

Because of the gunshots. That part of the night was crystal clear, although everything else was dark and fuzzy.

With Slade's help, she stood, and together they moved away from the river, into the wooded area. She tried to wring excess water from her wet clothes, but it was rather useless.

"We'll need to huddle together to help keep us warm." He pulled her close, sharing his warmth.

"Where's Colt?" She began to shiver again. There was plenty of wood around from various tree branches, and she wondered if Slade would start a small fire.

There was a pause before he said, "I'm not sure. I'm hoping he's behind us."

Slade was obviously concerned about his fellow marshal. She could certainly understand why and swallowed hard, wishing she understood what was going on.

When would her memory return? She'd hoped that when her headache eased, her brain would begin functioning normally again.

But that hadn't happened, yet.

She cleared her throat and tried not to dwell on her memory loss. "Colt will be here soon."

"I know. By the way, how's your headache?"

Slade's deep, husky voice was dangerously close to her ear.

"Better," she admitted, despite her continued shivering. She turned to look at him but couldn't read his expression in the faint moonlight. "Believe it or not, I think the cold water helped."

"I'm glad." His embrace was warm, and she instinctively cuddled closer.

She shivered again, despite his nearness. "Are you going to start a fire?"

"Not yet. I don't want to draw undue attention if someone is out there looking for us."

"For us? Or me?"

He hesitated, then said, "I'm not leaving you alone, Robyn. We're going to stick together from here on out."

Until when? Her memory had returned? And what if it didn't? Obviously Slade intended to protect her and hoped his efforts wouldn't be in vain.

She knew full well if she couldn't testify, then she was of no use to him.

"I'm sorry we had to escape another safe house," Slade said.

"It's not your fault." Her shivering was slowing down, and exhaustion pulled at her. She blinked, trying to stay awake. "I'm sorry I lost my memory."

"That's not your fault, either," Slade murmured.

Despite their dire circumstances, she found herself smiling.

They were both wet and cold, huddling together for warmth. This closeness she felt toward Slade wasn't anything more than two people depending on each other to stay alive.

No point in wasting time thinking about her handsome marshal. Her focus right now needed to be on regaining her memory.

Before whoever had attempted to kill her tried again.

Slade felt Robyn relax against him. He tucked her closer in an effort to share body heat.

Unfortunately, her skin was still cool to the touch, and he worried about hypothermia setting in. Cold, wet clothing would hasten its onset. He might have to risk a fire, despite their need to stay hidden.

He stared out at the river, wondering where Colt was. He'd felt certain his buddy had had time to get down over the ridge, but had something happened when he'd dropped into the river? Had Colt's head hit a rock, knocking him unconscious?

None of the scenarios flitting through his mind were reassuring. Colt was smart and athletic. Slade had to believe his friend would make it.

The idea of losing another colleague, especially one he was very close to, was unimaginable. The

US Marshal service had a great reputation for protecting their witnesses, and he knew that often meant putting their own lives on the line in order to accomplish their core mission.

But to lose two marshals in one case was highly unusual. How had Robyn's safe house been breached? Until he knew, they had to stay under the radar.

Trusting no one, other than Colt and Tanner, two marshals he'd worked closely with over the past few years.

Once he might have prayed to God for solace, but not anymore. He felt his eyes sliding closed and quickly forced them open. He needed to get that fire going.

A splash reached his ears.

He tensed and focused on the river. Colt? Or one of the bad guys?

Gently easing away from Robyn, he moved toward the riverbank. Another splash, and he caught a glimpse of a small head bobbing in the water.

Slade's heart pounded, and he continued moving closer to the edge of the river.

Had the cops followed them into the water? He still had his weapon, although drenched guns weren't known for their accuracy.

With uncharacteristic hesitation, he stared at the water, then saw a familiar face float by.

"Colt!" he shouted, despite the obvious need to be quiet.

The person in the water turned and waved seconds before disappearing from sight.

Stepping farther out on the riverbank, he craned his neck to see Colt making his way up and onto the shore. When his friend stood up, water running off him, a wave of relief hit hard.

Colt had made it!

Slade lifted his arm, waving madly. Colt headed toward him, dodging trees and rocks along the shoreline. Slade met him halfway and clapped him on the back.

"I'm so relieved you made it," Slade said softly.

"Was there any doubt?" Colt teased, although his pale skin and uncontrolled shivering belied his words. "You have Robyn?"

"Yeah. This way." Slade took Colt through the narrow path he'd made leading to the cocoon in the brush he'd tried to fashion to trap some warmth. He put his hand on Robyn, who stirred but then went lax, as if she'd fallen asleep. "I'm worried about her. She's probably suffering from hypothermia. I think we should risk starting a small fire."

Colt nodded in agreement.

Slade quickly got to work, piling dry leaves, sticks and branches in a clearing that was hopefully far enough from the river's edge that it couldn't be easily seen. Starting a fire without a lighter was a challenge, but he finally coaxed a small flame into a larger blaze. The warmth had Robyn instinctively edging closer.

"Colt is here?" she asked with a frown.

"Yeah." Slade was glad she remembered Colt. "Maybe we should have gone to the opposite bank," Slade said, staring off into the darkness.

"I think a bigger issue is where we go from here," Colt pointed out. "We don't have a vehicle, and our phones won't work now that they've been drenched in the river. Not to mention all of our money is sopping wet, as are our clothes."

No argument they were in a tough spot. Slade glanced up at the ridge behind them. "We'll have to climb the embankment to reach civilization. If we can get someone to lend us their phone, we can call Tanner."

Colt turned so that his back was to the fire, soaking up the warmth. "Tanner is our best option, but it's going to take time for him to get here. What are we going to do in the meantime?"

"I don't know," Slade admitted. He pulled off his sweatshirt and tried to dry it over the fire for Robyn to wear. "The only thing I know for certain is we're not going to the local police."

"Agreed," Colt murmured.

Robyn turned so that her back was to the fire, as well. Her shivering seemed better, and when she shifted position to face the fire again, her expression was one of relief.

The fire had been necessary, especially since they'd have to continue through the woods in their wet clothes. Hopefully his sweatshirt would help her stay warm. Hypothermia was nothing to take lightly.

"Why are the local police involved in this?" Robyn asked.

Slade exchanged a knowing glance with Colt. "Frankly, Robyn, we were hoping you might have an answer to that."

Her brow furrowed. "You mean, because of whatever I was going to testify about?"

Slade nodded but didn't want to say too much. He wanted her memory to return naturally, not because he filled the holes with pertinent details of the case.

It was bad enough that her amnesia compromised the entire trial. He felt certain that the team of lawyers defending Elan Gifford would pounce on her head injury like a wolf on raw meat.

A wave of frustration washed over him. He could testify and swear that he had not done anything to compromise Robyn's testimony, but would a jury believe him?

Over Elan Gifford's high-priced legal team?

He wasn't exactly thrilled about testing that theory. Better for Robyn to remember on her own, adding details that only she could know.

Especially related to whatever had sent her running from the safe house before she'd ended up at the bottom of the church basement stairs.

Robyn put a hand to her head. "I've been trying to remember, but everything is so blurry. Like I'm trying to see images through thick-lensed glasses."

"Try not to push so hard," Slade advised. There was no denying they didn't have much time, but he felt certain that forcing her to remember was counterproductive.

Her memory would return on its own.

He hoped.

"Hey, at least you remembered how to swim," Colt teased.

The corner of her mouth turned up in a lop-sided smile. "Yeah, but barely. I'm a runner, not a swimmer."

"You remember running?" Slade asked, trying to sound casual despite the thrill of anticipation.

"Yes," Robyn replied slowly. Her smile faded, and she frowned. "I think I must have done some track in high school or college, because I have a brief memory of running over a finish line."

Slade knew she was a runner but was keenly disappointed she hadn't remembered running with him over the past week. Instead, her memory had gone back to her college days.

She'd told him all about her track participation in college, claiming cross-country was her best event.

"That's great, Robyn," Colt encouraged. "See? You're already starting to remember. I agree with Slade, don't try to force it. Your memory will return in bits and pieces soon enough."

"I hope so," Robyn murmured.

It was the *soon enough* part that worried Slade. He fed another few dried sticks into the fire, hoping they weren't too noticeable.

"How far down the river do you think we made it?" Slade looked at Colt. "Any idea?"

His buddy hesitated for a moment. "I would say at least ten miles, maybe a little more."

Ten miles wasn't that far considering the police had vehicles at their disposal.

Then again, the highway didn't parallel the river, but wound around to various cities.

Still, he didn't like it. They weren't far enough from the Greeley safe house for his peace of mind.

"We'll need to start walking at dawn." He fed another stick into the fire. After some time passed, he felt the sweatshirt, believing it was dry enough for Robyn to wear. He gave it to her. "We won't look, but you need to take your wet shirt off and replace it with this."

"Okay."

Slade wished they could go up the embankment now, but scaling a ridge in the dark wasn't smart.

"Better?" he asked when Robyn returned.

"Much, thanks. Maybe we should go now?"

"I don't want to risk additional injuries." Slade knew Robyn was already suffering from amnesia. Adding broken bones to the mix wasn't smart.

"Yeah," Colt agreed. "Especially since we don't exactly know where we are."

"Not far enough away from Greeley, that's for sure," Slade said with a sigh.

"We could be closer to Garden City than you think," Robyn said.

He turned to stare at her. "You remember Garden City?"

She frowned. "I know it's south of Greeley, so it makes sense the river would take it in that direction."

"That's true," he said, trying to hide a stab of disappointment. "But I thought maybe you were familiar with the place on a personal level."

Robyn put a hand to her head again, and he felt guilty for pushing.

"Never mind," he amended quickly. "I hope you're right about being closer to Garden City than Greeley." Obviously Greeley as a safe house location hadn't worked out so well for them.

Garden City wasn't likely much better. Still too close for comfort.

Slade battled a wave of frustration. They needed a set of wheels and a new place to stay.

Suddenly a blinking light in the distance caught his attention. Slade reacted instantly, kicking up dirt to extinguish the fire.

"Shh," he warned, pulling Robyn close and placing her behind him.

The bobbing light flickered again, and he knew the source must be a flashlight.

Grimly, he realized the cops who'd come to the safe house were out there, searching for them.

FIVE

Robyn couldn't believe what a difference the small fire and wearing a warm sweatshirt made. Her brain had gotten foggy, but once she'd warmed up a bit, her thoughts cleared. She'd reveled in the heat radiating from the low flames until Slade abruptly put it out.

"What's wrong?" she whispered.

"Lights, in the distance. Those cops are searching for us." Slade's voice was low and grim. "We need to move."

"Move?" She glanced between Colt and Slade. "Where?"

"Away from here." Slade took her hand and helped her stand. "Stay quiet, okay?"

Heart in her throat, she nodded. The idea of the cops finding them was enough to scare her into silence.

Why was this happening?

Her temple throbbed as she did her best to follow Slade's footsteps. The nagging headache was still there, although thankfully with far less intensity than prior to being dunked in the icy river. Colt was behind her, and she was humbled by the way these two men were determined to keep her safe.

Thank You, Lord, for bringing these two marshals into my life.

As if by automatic reflex, the prayer echoed in her mind, and it took her a moment to realize she must have gone to the church on purpose.

Because she'd viewed it as a sanctuary. A place to be safe. A place to pray.

It was a piece of the puzzle that was her past life, and she clung to it with renewed hope. This must be a part of God's plan.

Slade led them along a path that followed the riverbank while keeping in the shadows as much as possible. When she tripped, Slade spun around to catch her.

"Okay?" he whispered.

"Yes."

His warm embrace was gone in a nanosecond, but she felt the impact for several minutes. Logically, she knew Slade viewed her as a job, a witness he needed to protect, but she couldn't help wondering about him.

Was he married? Did he have a family?

She hadn't seen a wedding ring, but that didn't

always mean much these days. Some men chose not to wear one, and some women, too.

Not her. She would want her husband to wear a ring, as she would.

Enough, she inwardly chided. What did it matter if Slade was married or not? She couldn't even remember her own past. What if she had a man in her life?

The thought brought her up short.

Surely, she'd remember a husband or a fiancé, wouldn't she?

Maybe, but maybe not.

"Slade?" Colt's low voice cut through the silence. "Hold up a sec."

Slade stopped, and turned to face them. "What's wrong?"

"Nothing, but I'd like to go up and over the edge of the ridge, see what's up top."

In the faint moonlight she could see Slade's scowl. "Why? The farther we go, the better."

"Depends on what's up there," Colt argued. "We need civilization, and what if we find ourselves far from a city? We'd just have to backtrack."

"Good point," Slade conceded. "Robyn and I will stay here, but if you don't return in a half hour, we're coming up to find you."

"No, if I don't return in a half hour, you'll get Robyn out of here," Colt corrected.

Slade reluctantly nodded. "Okay. Be careful."

Colt's smile flashed in the darkness. "Always am."

Robyn shivered as Colt moved past her to head up the slope of the ridge. It wasn't nearly as steep here, as it had been in Greeley where they'd gone over, but it still appeared hazardous.

Especially at night.

Slade must have noticed her shiver, because he drew her into the woods and helped her sit down. Moving had kept her warm, but now the wind seemed to sap her strength. Her legs were still freezing cold in the wet jeans. "We'll keep each other warm while we wait."

He wrapped his arm around her, and she immediately felt comforted by his presence. Colt was a nice man, too, but there was something about Slade that called to her on a deeper level.

A branch snapped. She flinched and jerked her head toward the sound.

"It's just Colt," Slade murmured, his breath warm in her ear. "We're safe."

Of course it was Colt. She glanced back the way they'd come. There was no sign of the bobbing flashlights.

Because the cops had turned them off, giving up the search? Or were they still out there?

Slade had agreed to give Colt thirty minutes,

and the minutes dragged by so slowly, she felt as if they'd been sitting twice that long.

"Any new memories?" Slade asked, his voice rumbling near her ear.

She shivered, from both the cold and being held in his arms. "Not really, although I know I attend church on a regular basis." She shrugged. "Praying comes naturally to me."

"That's great news." Slade tightened his arm around her in a brief hug. "I had a feeling you'd gone to the church in Timnath for a reason."

He had? She frowned. "You know more about me than I do. Why don't you fill in some of the blanks?"

He sighed. "Robyn, as much as I would love to do that, I need your memory to return naturally, not because I told you what you should remember."

"What difference does it make?" She was oddly irritated with his response.

"A huge difference when it comes to you testifying at trial," Slade said. "Gifford's defense attorney may claim you don't remember anything but are only repeating what you've been told. Don't you see? It's important you remember what you witnessed for yourself."

"Oh, I guess you're right." She grimaced at her foolishness. "I need to be able to say that I saw the guns in the boxes labeled 'furniture' because I did actually see them."

Slade froze. "You remember seeing guns in boxes labeled 'furniture'?"

She blinked and tried to focus on the hazy memory. "Yes, I do."

"That's wonderful news." Slade sounded as excited as if she'd given him a new car. "Can you remember anything else?"

Pulling up the image of the guns in the boxes, she tried to follow the slip of memory. What had she done after seeing them? Had she hidden away or reported it? Or had she taken pictures?

The memory faded, and she reluctantly shook her head. "No, sorry. It's just a memory fragment that floated through my brain, but there's nothing else I can pinpoint."

She sensed his keen disappointment, but he simply said, "That's okay, Robyn. You're doing great. Every memory that returns is important. It means your amnesia isn't permanent, which is a big deal."

"I'll keep trying, Slade," she promised. Although she didn't share his enthusiasm.

Oh, she wanted to remember, desperately, but one sliver of memory wasn't enough. And what had Slade mentioned? Something about the trial taking place in a few days?

She found it hard to believe the holes in her memory would be filled in that short of a time. Then again, she was no medical expert.

Maybe she should have that follow-up CT scan after all.

Another sound of a branch snapping came—followed by a scuffle of some sort. Slade tensed and eased away from her.

"Stay down," he whispered.

She scrunched down farther, edging beneath the brush. She willed herself not to shiver, her heart thudding painfully as she strained to listen.

After what seemed like a lifetime, she heard low voices.

"You okay?" Slade asked.

"Yeah" was Colt's response.

Colt was back. She let out a soundless sigh of relief and pushed upright.

The two men quickly joined her.

"What did you find?" Slade asked.

"There's some sort of building with a few cars scattered in the parking lot," Colt explained. "It's a business of some sort, but I can't tell you more because the sign was angled away from me."

"Okay, that's good news." Slade paused, then added thoughtfully, "Cars mean people and phones. We'll need to call Tanner, see how far away he is."

"Agreed." Colt glanced up at the sky. "Dawn should arrive soon. It's good that some cars are already up in the parking lot. Hopefully there will be more arrivals, and someone we can convince to allow us to use their phone."

"First we have to get up the ridge," Slade said wryly. "Robyn? How are you feeling?"

Both men were looking at her, so she forced a smile while trying to ignore another shiver. "Good. I'm fine. I'll be able to make it to the top."

She hoped.

"Okay, Colt, you're going to lead the way, since you already did this once. I'll stay behind Robyn, just in case."

Just in case what? To catch her if she fell and slid down the ridge?

Robyn blew out a breath, steeling her resolve.

Somehow, she'd find a way to make it up that ridge, no matter how difficult.

These men were putting their lives on the line for her. She needed to do her part rather than hold them back.

Slade waited for Colt to begin his trek back up to the top of the ridge. He hoped his buddy would avoid the slippery part that he'd hit on the way down.

The last thing they needed was for Robyn to hit her head again. Or break a limb.

Robyn did her best to follow Colt, and Slade was impressed with her sheer determination to get up the ridge. He stayed below her, though, ready to grab her if she fell.

Hearing how she remembered seeing guns in

boxes marked "furniture" was encouraging. Once they found another safe house, he'd find a way to convince her to follow up with a neurologist. Maybe there was something more they could do to help Robyn regain her lost memories.

Colt was obviously going slower, likely choosing a better path for Robyn's sake.

They were about halfway up when Robyn's foot slipped off a rock. He held his breath, preparing to grab her as she clung there for a moment, then regained her footing.

With a grim smile, he continued following her progress. It took them twice as long to reach the top, but when he saw Colt give Robyn a hand up, he blew out a sigh of relief.

Joining them up top, he raked his gaze over Robyn. She had a new scratch on her cheek but otherwise looked unharmed. "Good job," he told her quietly.

She smiled. "Thanks, but I don't think I'll be adding mountain climbing to my list of hobbies. Running provides all the endorphins I need."

Again, her reference to running offered surge of hope. But there wasn't time to question her further now.

As Colt had mentioned, there was a parking lot about twenty yards from them. What his buddy had failed to mention was the chain-link fence.

Not insurmountable, but far from encouraging.

He estimated the time was roughly seven in the morning, and there were already a dozen vehicles in the parking lot. Maybe a manufacturing type of place? Or maybe one of those large department stores?

Hard to say without knowing the name of the company.

A pair of headlights momentarily blinded him, and he ducked down, hoping Colt and Robyn had done the same. The lights belonged to a pickup truck and swept over them as the driver pulled into the parking lot.

"We have to climb the fence?" Robyn asked in a horrified whisper.

"'Fraid so," Colt responded. "There's a gate that moves from side to side allowing cars with badges to enter, but that will be too dangerous for us."

"Climbing up and over the fence isn't much better," Slade muttered. "I'll go first."

"No, let me," Colt argued. "Better that you stay here with Robyn. Maybe I can figure out how to open the gate for the two of you."

It went against the grain for Slade to leave everything to Colt, but there was no denying their mission was first and foremost to keep Robyn safe.

"Okay, go, then. But hurry." He wished they'd have gotten up here a little earlier, like before dawn. The sky was already light enough now that it would be easy for anyone looking this way to see Colt scaling the chain-link fence.

And if there were cameras on the building along with a security department and officers watching the video feeds? Even more of a challenge.

Colt sprang to his feet and lightly ran toward the fence.

"Please, God, watch over him," Robyn whispered.

Despite not having attended church as a parishioner in the past two years, Slade found himself silently echoing her prayer.

Colt was up and over the fence in minutes. He dropped down on the ground lightly, then ducked behind a large SUV. Slade braced himself for a security officer or two to show up, but nothing happened.

Colt began moving from car to car, looking inside and testing door handles. Most were locked, of course, but there was an older-model minivan that wasn't. He pulled out a white badge-like thing and carried it over to the gate.

"Let's go, Robyn." Slade was relieved she wouldn't have to climb the fence. They ran around to the now opening gate and hurried into the parking lot.

"Thanks, Colt." The gate closed behind them, and he glanced around hoping to see someone in the area.

But everyone was inside the building.

"We need to steal a car," Slade said. "Maybe the minivan."

Robyn's hand clutched his arm with surprising force. "Wait, what? We can't steal a van. That's illegal!"

"I know, Robyn." He covered her hand with his and tried to smile reassuringly. "Trust me, I wouldn't do this if it wasn't important. And the marshal service will reimburse the owner and take care of any extraneous expenses."

"But still, stealing?" Robyn looked truly distressed. "What if the owner of the van has a family, like young kids? There must be another way."

Slade glanced at the building and the other cars, evaluating. "The only other way would be to chance going in there—" he shrugged toward the doors of the complex "—and possibly run into more trouble if some security guard decides to call the police. Too risky."

"No car seats in the van," Colt said. "If there is a family, the kids are older than eight years old. Besides, Slade is right. The marshal service will make the owner whole. This will be a temporary inconvenience."

"Temporary inconvenience?" Robyn was not convinced. "It's a big deal, Slade."

He gazed down at her for a long moment. "So

is keeping you safe, Robyn. I need you to trust me on this, okay?"

Her anguished gaze tore at his heart, but then she nodded. He gave Colt the signal, and they quickly made their way to the minivan.

Newer models with key fobs and such were much harder to steal. Not that he was an expert. Thankfully, the minivan was at least fifteen years old and still used an old-fashioned key to start the engine. It didn't take long for Colt to crack open the casing beneath the steering wheel to reach the ignition wires.

"Get in the back." Slade opened the door for Robyn. "And keep your head down."

Thankfully Robyn did as he asked, despite her misgivings about their stealing the vehicle. And he understood where she was coming from.

The engine roared to life. Slade closed the door behind Robyn and ran around to get in beside Colt. He cranked the heat, grateful for the blast of warm air coming through the vents. They'd just gotten the van backed out of the parking spot when the sound of the gate opening reached his ears.

He tensed and glanced at Colt. His partner kept a benign expression on his face as he drove toward the gate. Slade held his breath as the incoming vehicle passed by.

From what he could tell, the driver didn't so much as glance at them.

"Hey, maybe we can use his phone to call Tanner," Robyn said from the back seat. "Then we wouldn't need to steal the van at all."

He briefly considered her suggestion but then shook his head. He turned to look at her. "Too risky," he repeated. "We're already in the van driving away and would have to explain why we hotwired it. All of which would likely cause the guy to call the police. And we know what happened the last time the local police got involved." That's why he'd opted for this plan rather than heading into the business itself to use someone's phone. Sopping wet, clearly on the run, they looked suspicious. For all they knew, local law enforcement had a BOLO out for them. He couldn't chance being detained by well-meaning security guards.

Robyn had nearly died. No way was he trying that again.

From this moment on, he was only going to trust Colt and Tanner.

At least until Robyn regained her memory.

He looked back at the parking lot and noticed the man staring after them, as if belatedly realizing the van shouldn't have been leaving the parking lot at all.

Did the guy know the owner?

Very likely.

"Hit the gas, Colt," he advised. "The cops might be on our tail sooner than expected."

Colt's expression was grim, and he punched the accelerator, sending the car up to highway speeds.

Slade swallowed hard. He'd hoped they'd have more time before being caught by the police.

But now they needed to improvise.

SIX

Robyn huddled in the back seat, glad for the warm air blasting through the vents but also horrified to know they'd stolen this vehicle.

She had never broken the law. Had she?

Hard to know for sure when she couldn't remember squat about her past.

The idea of stealing was abhorrent, though, so she decided to believe that this was a first for her. Yes, as Slade had pointed out, a necessity in order to stay alive.

Swallowing hard, she watched out the window as Colt picked up speed. It was impossible to relax; she kept waiting for the sound of police sirens.

Which didn't take long.

Their distant whine elevated the tension in the vehicle.

"Find a gas station," Slade said. "We need to find a phone, ASAP."

Colt grimaced, his gaze going frequently to the rearview mirror. "Don't you think we're better off putting more distance between us and the scene of the crime?"

Slade shifted in his seat, clearly torn. "I just wish we had a scheduled meeting spot with Tanner. Which we can't arrange until we talk to him."

"Give me some time," Colt told him.

Slade gave a curt nod, but Robyn could tell he wasn't happy. She couldn't blame him. The sirens were still faint, as if far away, but for how long?

Probably not very.

For long moments no one spoke. Finally Slade broke the silence. "We're heading for Loveland?"

"Yeah, why?" Colt glanced at him curiously.

"I think we're going to need to ditch the van somewhere and use a ride share or taxi service," Slade said slowly.

"Okay, we'll use the same tactic we did in Wyoming," Colt agreed.

"Wyoming?" She frowned. "Was that a different case?"

"Yes, nothing related to you, Robyn." Slade twisted in his seat to look at her. "Colt is going to drop us off somewhere with lots of people so we can borrow a phone. He'll ditch the van somewhere else, then meet back up with us."

It sounded reasonable, although anyone looking at them would be able to tell they'd been swimming in the river, and likely not by choice, considering it was mid-December. "We're still going to be noticeable."

"Yeah." Slade dug a wad of wet cash from his pocket. He held up several large-denomination bills in front of the heating vents. "A change of clothes and food will be high on the list, after we reach Tanner."

"Maybe before you try to call Tanner," Colt countered. "Robyn is right—looking like a couple of drowned rats is not a good way to inspire enough trust for a stranger to loan you a phone."

"Fine." Slade sighed and continued drying the money. "Although finding a store open this early might be a challenge."

Robyn's stomach rumbled with hunger, but she didn't voice the discomfort. At least her headache was better so that she didn't feel sick to her stomach.

Small blessings.

The sirens grew slightly louder, but they were nearly within the Loveland city limits. Robyn noticed a midsize plane lifting off, surprised the airport was large enough for commercial flights.

"There's a department store up ahead," Slade said. "Drop us off there."

"Got it." Colt turned off the highway and onto the street that led to the superstore. Cars were parked in the lot, which gave Robyn hope that the store might already be open.

"Where do you want to meet?" Colt asked as he stopped to let them out. "The breakfast restaurant? It's not far from here."

"Sounds good." Slade slid out of the van and opened her door for her. Her jeans were still pretty wet, and the cool winter breeze made her shiver.

Slade slid his arm around her waist as they walked inside. Colt drove off with the van, and she hoped he would be okay as he found a place to leave it.

Then she frowned. "I thought the marshals were going to help make sure the owner was compensated?"

"Colt will get the VIN and the license plate, don't worry." He glanced at her. "Trust me on this, okay?"

She decided to let it go. The store was just opening up, so they were the first customers inside. Several store clerks gave them curious glances, but no one stopped them.

It didn't take long to purchase personal items and replacement clothing, including lightweight winter jackets. Slade included replacement items for Colt, too. They changed in the store restrooms, and when Robyn emerged ten minutes later she felt a hundred percent better. Being warm felt wonderful, and ironically her headache was far less painful, too.

She'd done her best to rinse the river water from

her hair, drying it by using the hot-air hand dryers. It wasn't the same as a shower, but better than nothing.

Slade was waiting for her, his hair damp from being rinsed. "It's wonderful to be dry," she said in a low voice. "Thank you."

"For me, too," Slade agreed. "Time to eat and find a phone."

Outside, she frowned at the silence. "What happened to the police sirens? Is Colt okay?"

"He'll be fine." Slade took her hand, holding on to the store bag with the other. "Walk casually as if we have nothing to hide."

She pasted what she hoped was a carefree smile on her face as they walked the few blocks to the breakfast restaurant. It was difficult not to glance over her shoulder, searching for signs of danger.

When they arrived at the restaurant, she noticed there were several families and a few older couples. Now that they were here, their plan to borrow a cell phone to call Tanner made her apprehensive.

"Table for three, please," Slade told the young hostess. "We have a friend joining us."

"Right this way." The young woman grabbed three menus and led the way to a booth.

"Could I ask a huge favor?" Slade said as the young woman set the menus down. "I dropped my phone, shattering it to smithereens, and need to call my friend. May I borrow yours? It will only take a minute."

Standing next to him, Robyn tensed, feeling certain the woman would tell him to take a hike, but surprisingly she pulled out her phone and handed it over.

"I hate when that happens," the young woman said. "Do you know how many paychecks I had to save up to buy a new one when I dropped mine? It was weeks before I was able to replace it."

"I hear you," Slade said, inputting the phone number. "It's very frustrating not to be able to connect with your friends over something as simple as meeting up for breakfast." He took a step away as he began talking softly into the phone.

"How long have you worked here?" Robyn asked, trying to divert the woman's attention from Slade's call.

"Just over two years," the young woman said. "I've decided to go back to college starting in January. No way am I working in a restaurant for the rest of my life."

"That's wonderful. Which university are you planning to attend?" She didn't dare glance at Slade, who was taking longer on the call than one would expect if he was truly just calling to have someone meet them. "Boulder?"

The woman nodded. "Yes. I spent one semester

there, then dropped out. Stupid mistake, right? I should have stuck it out."

"It's never too late to get an education," Robyn said. "And Boulder has a nice campus, better really than the University of Denver."

And how did she know that? She frowned, trying to remember when she'd been to Boulder. Or the University of Denver, for that matter. So frustrating to have these brief flashes of memory without any context.

What subjects had she studied, anyway?

"Thanks so much," Slade said warmly as he returned their hostess's phone. "I really appreciate your help."

"No problem." The young woman smiled, then turned when more customers entered the restaurant. "Your server, Janice, will be with you shortly."

"Thanks." Robyn slid into the booth, nonplussed when Slade took the spot next to her.

"Tanner is guarding a judge in Cheyenne and can't leave," Slade whispered in a low voice. "But he's arranging a rental car for us here in Loveland. The lot is nearby."

"That's good news." She should have realized Slade had only sat next to her so they could talk without anyone overhearing. She needed to get her wild emotions under control. "When will the rental car be ready?"

"In an hour, maybe less. But we'll eat first."

She nodded and looked down at the menu. The enticing scents of bacon and coffee were making her mouth water.

Janice arrived with three water glasses and a harried smile. "Coffee while you wait?" she asked.

"Yes, please," Slade said. "And we may go ahead and order. We're not sure when our friend will get here."

"That's fine. I'll get your coffee."

"Don't you think we should wait for Colt?" she whispered.

Slade shrugged. "I think it's going to take him a while. May as well eat while we wait."

"What makes you think that?" Robyn had assumed Colt would leave the car just a few blocks away, in some public parking lot.

Slade waited until Janice returned with two mugs of steaming coffee and had taken their order before answering. "Because knowing Colt, he'll leave the car at the airport, hoping not only that it will take them longer to find it, but also might convince them we left the city via plane."

Cradling her mug between her hands, she took a sip, thinking about what he'd said. "Pretty smart," she admitted.

"We marshals have our moments," Slade said dryly. Then his expression softened. "We'll keep you safe, Robyn."

"I know." Ridiculous tears pricked her eyes, and she subtly swiped them away. Silly to be weepy now that they were warm, dry and about to eat for the first time in twelve hours.

She only hoped and prayed her memory would return, making all of this effort worthwhile.

She couldn't bear the thought of letting Slade down.

Slade tried not to let his nervousness show. Robyn was tense enough after they'd stolen the van—he didn't want to add to her anxiety.

But for all his brave words, he'd expected Colt to be here by now. Even if he had left the van at the airport, it wasn't that far away.

He told himself that Colt would be here soon. And once they'd had breakfast, they'd pick up the rental car and get out of town for good.

In the meantime, they needed to eat. He could hear Robyn's stomach protesting the lack of food.

They'd just gotten their meals when Colt entered the restaurant. Slade waved him over and gave him the bag. "Change first. Do you want me to order something for you?"

"Coffee, three eggs over easy with wheat toast and bacon, thanks." Colt disappeared into the restroom.

He glanced at Robyn, who was sitting with her

hands clasped, her head bowed in prayer. He felt bad for talking to Colt while she was praying.

And had to resist the urge to join her.

Lately, he'd found it hard believe in the power of prayer. Too many losses had convinced him that God had either given up on him or had never been there at all.

But old habits were hard to break, so he sat quietly until she'd finished.

"I'm so glad Colt arrived," Robyn murmured as she picked up her fork and dug into her food. "I'm thinking the sooner we get out of Loveland, the better."

"Agree." Slade gestured for Janice to come over, repeating Colt's order.

Janice left, returning with a third mug of coffee at the same time Colt emerged from the bathroom.

"Everything okay?" Slade asked.

Colt sipped his coffee, let out a satisfied groan and nodded. "Yeah. Hopefully the airport location distracts them long enough for us to get out of here."

Slade nodded thoughtfully, making short work of his meal. "I wish I knew how they found the safe house."

"Which one?" Colt asked wryly.

"Both," Slade admitted. "I don't like it. There

must be a leak somewhere. This all spiraled downhill after I called our boss, James Crane."

Colt eyed him over the rim of his cup. "There hasn't been a corrupt marshal in years," he pointed out. "And Crane is a decent guy. Hard to imagine someone within the service has abruptly turned criminal."

"Wait a minute, you really think that someone within the marshal service is responsible?" Robyn asked, her eyes wide with fright. "How could that happen?"

"We don't know anything for sure," Slade said in an attempt to smooth things over. No reason to point out that anyone could be turned by greed, especially if the price was right. Robyn had been through enough in the past twenty-four hours. "We're just brainstorming possibilities, that's all."

She still looked troubled but didn't say anything more.

"Gifford has a lot of money," Colt said. "Could be he hired someone to infiltrate the marshal office and somehow tracked Crane's phone."

A few minutes later, Colt's breakfast arrived and they were all too busy eating to talk. But the possibility that it was his call to Crane that had somehow leaked their location nagged at him.

"Is Tanner coming through for us?" Colt asked.

"Sort of. He's guarding a judge and can't leave.

As soon as you're finished eating, we'll pick up the rental he's arranged for us." Slade glanced at Robyn, who was cradling her coffee to her chest as if she were still chilled. "You okay?"

"Fine." Her smile was wan. "I just wish I could remember more about Gifford."

He wished that, too, but didn't point out the obvious. "You will. For now, let's concentrate on getting out of town."

Colt finished his meal in record time, blotting his face with his napkin. "Can we take coffee to go?"

"Sure." Slade caught Janice's eye and pulled out his still-damp cash. He'd dried more of it while in the bathroom earlier. He had a debit card all deputy marshals were given for expenses, but he wasn't willing to take a chance on using it.

At least, not yet.

"We'll take three coffees to go, and the bill," Slade said when Janice returned. "Thank you."

"No problem."

"Where are we headed next?" Robyn asked as they waited. "Denver?"

Slade glanced at Colt, who shrugged. "It's not a bad idea."

Robyn looked confused. "I don't understand."

"The location of the trial is in Denver," Slade explained. "It's also where the crime you witnessed took place. Maybe being in Denver would help spark your memory."

She frowned, but nodded. "Okay, that sounds good."

Her easy acceptance to return to the place where all this started bothered him. Clearly Robyn didn't remember how desperate and afraid she'd been by the time they'd taken over the case.

If not for the fact that they needed her testimony to put Gifford away, he'd have preferred not to make her relive that fear.

But there wasn't another option. Colt was right. The best chance of prodding a return of her memory was to go back to where it all began.

He paid the bill and the three of them carried out their coffee, with Colt shouldering the bag of personal items. Slade led the way to the rental car agency, which happened to be a stone's throw away from the superstore.

"Smart move to pick up disposable phones," Colt said as they walked. "Now all we need is power and a phone to activate them."

"I was thinking we'd stop at a hotel at some point." Slade shrugged. "If we can find one that will take cash based on our badge."

"I'm sure we'll find something," Colt agreed.

Robyn huffed. "Not in downtown Denver, you won't. First of all, the prices are astronomical, especially this close to the holiday, and secondly, I highly doubt any of them will take cash."

Another memory? Slade glanced at her, trying to sound casual. "You're right about downtown Denver, but there must be plenty of places we can try on the outskirts of town."

Robyn frowned without saying anything, and his balloon of hope deflated.

"There may be a place on the east side of town," Robyn finally said. "I can't remember the name of it, though."

"We'll check it out," Slade promised, encouraged once again by the glimmers of memory. "Maybe you'll recognize it when you see it."

Once they arrived at the rental car place, he turned to Colt. "Wait here with Robyn, okay?"

"Sure." Colt shifted the bag from one hand to the other. "We'll be fine."

Slade nodded and hurried inside to produce his badge and driver's license, soggy as it was, to obtain the car. It was a black SUV, which was perfect.

The process didn't take long, and soon they were back on the road. The agency had provided a map, which he handed to Colt. "Looks like we take I-25 all the way to Denver. GPS will probably confirm."

When they passed the airport, several squad

cars came roaring past them, lights flashing as they raced into the airport parking lot.

Slade tightened his grip on the steering wheel, shocked they'd found the stolen van so quickly.

What if the men determined to silence Robyn also assumed they'd return to Denver?

He pressed on the accelerator, picking up speed. They needed to stay at least a couple of steps ahead of these guys.

A feat that was more difficult than he'd ever imagined.

SEVEN

Robyn blanched upon seeing the police cars rushing into the airport parking lot. Slade was headed in the opposite direction, leaving the cops behind. Still, a deep wave of dread washed over her, which didn't make any sense.

Police officers helped citizens, didn't they? Why this instinctive recoil from the local law enforcement authorities?

It didn't add up, but the sensation was too strong to be ignored. Maybe it had something to do with the holes in her memory.

"Don't forget the marshals are supposed to reimburse the van owner," she said.

"Our boss will take care of it, but not until we have you someplace safe," Slade said firmly.

"Do you think we'll be safe in Denver?" She wished the hot coffee was enough to ward off the shiver of fear. "Maybe we should try Boulder instead."

Slade met her gaze in the rearview mirror. "We're hoping Denver sparks your memories."

She grimaced and nodded. Going to Denver was the right thing to do, but that didn't mean she was looking forward to the trip. Which was strange. She wanted to remember her past.

Didn't she?

Finishing her coffee, she tucked the empty container in the cup holder. She rubbed her temples, wishing the lingering headache would go away. As soon as the thought landed, she pushed it aside.

Wallowing in self-pity wasn't her style. Time for her to count her blessings. She was alive and relatively unharmed. Her headache was way better than it had been. She had Slade and Colt, two US marshals, helping to keep her safe.

God was certainly watching over her; she needed to focus on remaining positive. Her memory would return in time to testify.

"Try not to force it," Slade advised. She dropped her hands to her lap and met his gaze. "Maybe just close your eyes and let your mind drift. See what memories float to the surface."

Robyn sighed and closed her eyes, resting her head in the corner between the cushion and the door. She tried to keep her mind blank, imagining she was looking up at a dark, starry sky.

Tired, so tired. Her muscles relaxed for what felt like the first time in eons. For sure since she'd woken up staring at a stranger.

Slade. Not a stranger. When had they met?

She couldn't remember.

Her attempt to clear her mind only resulted in her falling asleep.

She woke an hour later, when the SUV came to a stop. She blinked and looked around in confusion. "Where are we?"

"A small motel outside Denver." Slade turned to look at her. "You slept the entire way."

"Sorry." She flushed. "Guess clearing my mind put me to sleep."

"It's good you were able to get some rest." Slade glanced at Colt. "I know it's early in the day, and they may not let us check in until later, but see if you can get connecting rooms."

Colt nodded and slid out from the passenger seat.

Robyn looked around curiously, but nothing seemed remotely familiar. The motel was small and not far from the interstate. From what she could tell, she'd never been here before.

Then again, would she remember a place like this? Not likely.

In the distance she could see the Denver skyline, which in comparison was comfortably familiar, like an old sweater. She was encouraged by the feeling of coming home.

Maybe this idea of sparking memories would work.

Colt returned holding up two keys. He slid into the passenger seat. "Last two rooms on the lower level. Despite being so close to the holiday, they're not that busy, so she gave us an early check-in."

Robyn wasn't expecting much, so the dim interior holding a somewhat musty smell of the connecting rooms wasn't disappointing. The bathroom was clean, and she eyed the shower with envy. Her attempt to wash her hair in the restroom had been feeble at best.

"Do I have time to clean up?" she asked upon returning to the main room, where Colt had set the bag of personal items.

"Sure," Slade agreed. "I need to activate our new phones anyway, so take your time. When you're ready, we'll drive around a bit, see if anything looks familiar."

An hour later, she emerged from the bathroom feeling a hundred percent better. Hearing deep voices coming from the connecting room, the door hanging ajar, drew her over.

She rapped on the partially open door before crossing the threshold. "I'm ready when you are."

"Great." Slade jumped to his feet, and she could tell both men had made use of the time to clean up, as well. Slade pulled one of the small phones off the charger and tossed it to Colt. He took the other for himself. "Let's go."

Leaving the relative safety of the motel room gave her a tiny pang, but she knew it had to be done. "Denver traffic will be a bear," she said as Slade headed toward the skyline.

"You remember driving in it?" Slade asked casually.

A very brief flash of being stuck in traffic flitted through her mind, but it was gone so fast she couldn't be sure it was real, or something she might have seen on TV.

"Not really," she acknowledged. "Do I have a car?"

Slade shrugged but didn't answer. He had mentioned it would be better for her to remember on her own rather than hearing details about her life from him.

The memory of the guns in the boxes marked "furniture" was real. Of that she was certain. The image evoked a sick dread, as if she had somewhat expected to see something so awful.

Slade exited the highway in Thornton. She frowned, sitting up straighter in her seat. "This looks familiar," she murmured.

Slade and Colt exchanged a glance but didn't say anything. When Slade took another turn, she caught a glimpse of a sign in the distance.

"Gifford Furniture." She wondered why she hadn't put two and two together before now. "The place where I saw the guns in boxes labeled 'furniture' with subheadings of 'end tables and chairs.'"

"End tables and chairs?" Slade echoed. "You didn't mention that level of detail before."

"I didn't?" She could see the words now as if they were stamped in her brain. "Sorry about that." The Gifford Furniture sign was growing larger now as Slade approached. But the building itself appeared to be deserted. No lights were on inside, and there was a large Closed sign on the door.

"I must have worked there," she said mostly to herself. "Otherwise how would I have seen the guns?"

"Do you remember what you did there?" Slade asked.

She frowned, trying to conjure up more memories. She could remember walking into the store and heading to a small office with a computer on the desk. There had been a very small Christmas tree in the corner. "I think I was the manager."

"You were," Slade confirmed, a wide grin splitting his features. "See, being among familiar surroundings is working."

"I guess so. Do you know where I live?"

Slade hesitated and glanced at Colt. "What do you think? Gifford might have people staked out watching her place."

Colt grimaced. "They might, but the benefit of Robyn's memory returning outweighs the risk. Maybe we just cruise by, one SUV among dozens of others."

Slade nodded slowly. "Okay, thankfully it's not far."

The two-story row of apartments wasn't what she'd expected. Then again, housing located this close to Denver would be super expensive. This was obviously the best she could afford.

Unfortunately, seeing the building didn't help bring additional memories to the forefront of her mind. She had the impression she didn't spend a lot of time there.

"What are my hobbies?" she asked. Then, before either of the marshals could answer, she saw a church. "There!" She pressed her hand to the window. "I attend church services there!" Christmas hymns floated through her mind, making her smile.

"You do, and I'm glad your memory is returning." Slade hesitated, then added, "Do you remember anything else about the church?"

Her smile faded, wondering what he was getting at, then latched onto a fleeting image. A guitar and a microphone. Laughter and joy.

"Choir practice," she said breathlessly. "I—I'm part of the church choir. We were practicing for Christmas services."

Slade's smile widened. "Good job. I'm sure the rest of your memories will soon follow."

"I hope so." She glanced from the church to her apartment building. "Interesting that the church holds better memories for me than the place I live."

"Maybe not," Slade countered. "I mean, day-to-day types of activities like eating and sleeping aren't very memorable compared to activities you enjoy doing."

"Like being in the church choir." There was something about spending time at the church that nagged at her. But she couldn't pinpoint it. She shrugged it off.

It was a relief to know that her head injury was getting better.

Now if she could remember exactly what she needed to testify about, she'd be even more reassured.

The thought of anyone getting away with illegally selling guns was distressing. Especially if she was the only one who could help stop them.

Slade was thrilled at the progress they'd made with Robyn's memory. Returning to Denver had proved to be the right idea.

"Any suggestions on where else we can take her?" He glanced at Colt. "Her mother's house, maybe?"

"Not yet," Colt said cautiously. "We really don't

know where Gifford's men are, and I would feel bad if we somehow drew her mother into danger."

Colt was right, but it was depressing all the same. "We need a computer and replacement weapons. Call Tanner, see if he can secure them for us though the Denver office. I don't want to waste all our cash buying new stuff."

"Okay." While Colt made the call, Slade drove around the block, wondering if he should drive into the downtown area or back to the motel.

"Tanner arranged for a computer and replacement weapons, but he mentioned our boss is upset and wants to hear from you in particular, ASAP," Colt said with a sigh.

"Great," Slade muttered. The last time he'd called James Crane, Robyn's safe house had been compromised. Before that, Wainwright had been murdered. Although he couldn't imagine his boss was involved in any way, the timing still bugged him. "Let's find a place to pull over to make the call."

Five minutes later he was in a strip mall parking lot. Bracing himself, he called his boss's number, hoping Crane wouldn't answer because Slade was using a disposable phone.

But no, his boss answered on the first ring, shouting into his ear, "Brooks! Where have you been?"

"Bring it down a notch, I'm not deaf." Slade held

the phone several inches from his ear. "There's no need to yell."

"Yell?" If anything, Crane turned the volume up ten notches. "I don't appreciate my deputy marshals going off the grid and missing check-ins."

"I'm sorry, but our second safe house location was compromised, as well. We went over the ridge and down into the river, which trashed our phones." Slade glanced at Colt, who grimaced. "We just activated our new devices."

"And our witness?" Crane barked in a slightly mollified tone.

"Is fine, thanks for asking." Slade knew he should tone down the sarcasm, but it wasn't easy. "We're safe."

For now.

There was a moment of silence, then his boss said, "Glad to hear it. What is going on? How is it that these safe houses are being found?"

"I wish I knew," Slade said wryly. He didn't want to tell his boss about Robyn's amnesia, especially since he was hoping her memory would be fully restored, soon. "We ended up stealing a van. Colt has the VIN. You'll have to reimburse the owner as soon as possible."

Crane sighed. "Fine. Anything else?"

"No. We'll try to stay in touch, okay?"

"Yeah, yeah. If you could arrest one of the men

coming after Robyn, it would help put another nail in Gifford's coffin."

In between dodging bullets? Slade barely refrained from rolling his eyes. "We'll see what we can do."

Another pause. "Nelson is with you?"

"Yes." He didn't mention how Tanner had helped, too. Crane would find out when the car rental bill, the computer and replacement weapons hit their expense account. "Anything else, boss?"

"Stay in touch." Crane disconnected from the call.

"Is he always so crabby?" Robyn asked.

"Only when things are going wrong." Slade handed Colt the phone. "Let's get over to the office for the computer and guns. Maybe Robyn seeing more of the city will help."

"Okay, but drop me off a few streets from the place, just in case." Colt ran his fingers through his short blond hair. "Wish I had my cowboy hat."

"Me, too." Unfortunately, both hats were likely floating down the Poudre River, ending up who knows where.

The traffic was as lousy as always; the only bright spot was the Christmas lights stretching from light pole to light pole. It was during times like this that Slade missed where he'd grown up, a small town in Texas. There were only a few streets, and traffic would normally only stop for cattle or other live animals, rarely other vehicles.

His job as a US marshal took him between states, most recently Wyoming and Colorado. The Rocky Mountains were stunning, but he still preferred the wide-open spaces Texas had to offer.

At least, he had preferred them. It occurred to him that he hadn't returned to his hometown since losing Marisa.

Two years should have been long enough to get over her death, but he hadn't even been attracted to another woman until meeting Robyn.

He glanced at her in the rearview mirror. Robyn's pale skin and straight blond hair were completely opposite from Marisa's dark skin and curly black hair. Marisa had also gone to church regularly, which was why he'd avoided attending services after her death.

Leukemia had taken her before her thirtieth birthday.

"Hey, the Botanical Gardens," Robyn said in surprise. "I've been there several times."

Slade pulled his thoughts from his painful past. "Anything in particular stand out?"

"I loved seeing the beautiful flowers." Her tone was wistful. "But I don't remember who I was with."

Slade reminded himself that any memory was better than nothing.

He noticed Robyn's gaze followed the sign for the Botanical Gardens as they went by. The melancholy expression on her face made him feel as if her memories of the place were bittersweet.

Was that why she was having trouble remembering? He didn't recall her being super sad about anything when they'd gone on their runs together.

Oh, she'd been upset and angry about the assault rifles she'd found as they'd discussed the case against Gifford, but not sad.

He knew a lot about Robyn's background—the marshal service had dug into it—but he hadn't shared much with her about his personal life.

"It's a beautiful place to have professional photos taken," Robyn said thoughtfully.

He exchanged another glance with Colt. "You've had photos taken there?"

"I think so." Robyn's brow was furrowed as she struggled to remember. "It's foggy, though, as if I'm still peering through thick glass that's distorting the image."

Engagement photos. He knew she'd been briefly engaged but had recently broken up from that relationship.

"I'm glad the city is helping your memory," he said meeting her gaze in the rearview mirror.

"I guess." Robyn glanced away. "But real memories rather than these fragments that float by would be far more helpful."

He understood her frustration.

"Let me off here," Colt said as he stopped at a red light. "The Denver office is just a few blocks from here. I'll get there faster by foot."

Before Slade could respond, Colt jumped from the SUV, slamming the door shut behind him.

"I can't remember if I thanked you for saving my life," Robyn said quietly. "I owe you and Colt a true debt of gratitude, one I'll never be able to repay."

"You did thank us, although it's not necessary." When the light turned green, he inched forward, moving at a snail's pace. "We all want Gifford to pay for his crimes."

"Yes, we do." She frowned again, as if there might be another memory hanging just out of reach.

His phone rang, startling them both. Slade inwardly groaned when he recognized his boss's number.

Bracing himself, he answered, "Brooks."

"What happened in Greeley?"

"What do you mean?" Slade tried not to sound too exasperated. He shouldn't be talking on his cell phone while driving, so he looked around for a spot to pull over to avoid a cop stopping him and issuing a ticket. "I told you, our safe house was compromised and we escaped by going over the ridge and sliding down into the Poudre River."

"You didn't say anything about gunfire," Crane shot back. "Or injuring a cop."

"What?" Slade tucked the phone between his shoulder and his ear and pulled into a parking garage, then remembered. "Okay, listen, two cops came to the safe house, one in the front and one heading around back, both carrying their weapons as if ready to use them. There was no reason for them to be there, so we took off through the backyard toward the river. Colt provided cover while I took Robyn over the ridge."

"Well, he injured a cop, and the Greeley police want Colt charged for shooting an officer."

"How did they know we were marshals? I'll tell you how, because they're dirty cops," Slade insisted. "They would have shot and killed us all if we hadn't escaped."

There was a charged moment of silence. "Anything else you care to explain?"

Slade drew his hand over his face, trying to think through his exhaustion. "No, sir."

Another pause. "I'll stall the locals, but next time you shoot at a cop, consider letting me know."

Crane disconnected from the call. Slade sighed and glanced at Robyn, who had heard everything. Hard not to when his boss tended to shout loud enough for anyone in the vicinity to hear.

He didn't like this new wrinkle. Not one bit. It was a problem the cops had known they were marshals. It was almost as if the dirty cops were using this as a way to flush them out of hiding.

Not going to happen. Not on his watch. He'd protect Robyn with his life, no matter what they threw at him.

EIGHT

Robyn hated the idea of Slade and Colt being in trouble with their boss, but what could she do? Other than corroborate their story.

Not that the idea of providing more testimony in a court of law held any appeal. That's what had gotten her into this mess.

On the heels of that thought came a flash of shame. What was she thinking? Of course she needed to testify against Gifford; it was the right thing to do. She was in danger now only because the bad guys didn't want her to testify. They were hoping to scare her off.

No, not just scare her off. Silence her, forever.

The grim thought brought a renewed determination. These people needed to be stopped. Who knew how many other innocent people had been hurt as a result of their crimes?

And if anyone could keep her safe throughout this, it would be Slade.

She had complete and utter faith in him. And knowing God was watching over them helped, too.

"There's Colt," Slade said breaking into her thoughts.

She saw Colt with a computer bag over his shoulder, threading his way through the pedestrians to reach their vehicle. Within moments, he'd slid into the passenger seat, setting the computer on the floor at his feet.

After waiting for a break in traffic, Slade pulled out of the parking lot and glanced at Colt. "Our boss is not happy with us," he said bluntly. "Apparently one of your shots back in Greeley wounded a cop."

Colt grimaced. "I had no idea. I was simply shooting in the direction the gunfire was coming from."

"I know," Slade said wearily. "They want you in custody, but Crane is going to stall the locals at least long enough to get through the trial."

"And the trial is in four days?" Robyn asked. "I'm trying to keep track."

"Yes." Slade met her gaze in the rearview mirror. "But don't worry about it. The first day of a trial is mostly picking a jury in a process called voir dire. You likely won't testify until the second day."

She nodded, although wasn't sure one extra day

mattered. Her memory needed to return before the trial, and the sooner the better.

Colt glanced skeptically at Slade but didn't say anything. She understood what he was thinking—that they'd have to tell the DA about her memory issues before the trial started.

She gazed at the cheerful Christmas decorations, wishing she could experience her usual joy at the upcoming holiday, rather than dreading the looming trial.

Nearly an hour later they were back inside their connecting rooms. Colt carried the computer case to the room he and Slade shared, setting it on the table. He handed Slade a gun, took one for himself, then pulled out the computer and turned it on. For several minutes there was nothing but silence as they waited for the computer to sync up with the motel's free Wi-Fi signal.

There was a nervous flutter in her stomach as Colt brought up the website of Gifford Furniture with a couple of keystrokes. "Does this help?"

When Colt moved aside, she sat down and peered at the images. The interior of the store looked very familiar but did not spark additional memories. "I kinda remember being in the store, but nothing specific. No arguments or discussions of any kind." She shrugged and glanced up at Slade. "I was the store manager, right?"

He nodded. "Yes."

She returned her gaze to the screen. "It might be helpful for me to see my office, rather than just the furniture itself."

"I know, but it's too dangerous to go there now," Slade said. "Colt, see if you can pull up any pictures of her family."

"I thought you wanted me to remember on my own?" she asked.

"I do, but we're running out of time. Your family isn't part of the trial, so we should be okay."

Colt turned the computer toward him so he could work.

"I'm on social media?" Her voice hitched a bit. "Isn't that risky?"

Slade's hand was warm on her shoulder. "We've taken all your social media down, Robyn, but we have a few pictures we saved during our initial investigation."

For some weird reason, the knot in her stomach tightened. She subconsciously held her breath when a photograph popped up on the screen.

It was a picture of herself as a teenager, with two younger guys standing on each side of her. They looked maybe a year or two younger than she was, even though they were both much taller.

"Nothing?" Slade asked.

She stared at it for a long time, then blew out a breath of annoyance. "It looks familiar, but I can't tell you who those two kids are."

"They are your stepbrothers, Leon and Joey."

Leon and Joey. She rolled the names around in the vacant spot in her brain. Shouldn't step-brothers be easy to remember? She turned away to look up at Slade. "Do you have photographs of my parents?"

"No, sorry." Slade held her gaze. "Your mother's name is Lucille."

"Lucille Lowry," she murmured. A sense of desolation hit hard. Even worse than not remembering her stepbrothers was forgetting her own mother. Then she frowned. "What about my father?"

Slade shook his head. "You told me your father wasn't involved in your life. Your parents were divorced when you were young, and your mom remarried a man named George Lowry, who had two young boys from a previous marriage."

George and Lucille Lowry. She closed her eyes and tried to relax, hoping a picture of them would flash in her mind.

But it didn't.

There was something familiar about the two boys' young faces, though. She opened her eyes and studied the photograph again. It wasn't a great picture; they were in the sun and they were squinting at the brightness, so it wasn't easy to read the expressions in their eyes.

"I don't understand why I don't have pictures of my mom," she said.

"To be fair, you may have them at your apartment. We pulled this off your social media page before shutting it down, but you actually didn't post much on any of the social media sites. There were some photographs of you singing in the church choir, and there is one other one, too." Slade gestured to Colt, who once again worked the computer screen.

The picture that bloomed on the screen was a close-up of Robyn and a man about two inches taller than her, with longish blond hair and a lopsided smile.

"Dale Jones." The name popped instantly into her mind. And the background of the photograph clicked in her brain, too. "Our engagement photo. This was taken at the Botanical Gardens."

"That's correct." Slade hesitated, then asked, "Anything else?"

"Dale broke off our engagement recently." She remembered the feeling of shocked surprise when Dale had told her things just weren't working out for him. "He claimed I was boring and only interested in church activities."

Slade's hand tightened comfortingly on her shoulder. "I know, and I'm sorry, but he sounds like a jerk."

That made her smile. It was heartening to know that church and faith were a part of her life. And that Slade was supportive of her.

But she still didn't remember everything about her past. Like her family.

Colt moved away, and she continued staring at the photograph of her standing with her stepbrothers. The idea that she couldn't remember her own family made her feel awful.

Tears pricked her eyes. She swiped them away and then pushed from the table. "Excuse me."

She rushed through the doorway connecting their rooms, trying to rein in her emotions. Logically she knew the injury her brain had sustained wasn't her fault. It wasn't as if she was blocking the memories from resurfacing.

But not remembering her mother?

"Robyn?" Slade's hands cupped her shoulders. "It's okay. Try not to stress out over this."

She let out a strangled laugh, sniffed and wiped at her eyes again. "It's hard not to, knowing my mother is out there somewhere…" She couldn't finish.

Slade gently turned her and hauled her close. Unable to resist the offer of comfort, she hid her face against his chest and took several deep breaths in an attempt to relax.

This was just a minor setback. She'd remembered Dale, and she didn't even like him very much anymore. Surely she'd remember her mother and her stepbrothers soon.

Slade's embrace warmed her from head to toe,

and for a moment she wished she'd never have to leave his arms.

Silly to want something like that, when she knew very well that he was just being nice to help her regain her memory.

Slade pressed a chaste kiss to her temple. It was proof of how much an emotional wreck she was when the sweet gesture almost had her dissolving once again in tears.

She told herself to *buck up, buttercup*. Steeling her resolve, she lifted her head, smiled and pulled out of his arms.

"Thanks, Slade. I'm fine. Maybe a bit over-tired."

"Completely understandable." His green gaze was so intense, she had a hard time tearing away. "Why don't you try to get some rest?"

She shook her head. "I think it's better if we continue finding ways to spark my memory. What we've been doing so far seems to be working. At least a little."

"Later, after lunch," Slade suggested. "Get some rest. We have a little work to do on our end."

What kind of work? She was curious but didn't ask. Slade headed back through the connecting doorway to his room, and it took every ounce of willpower she had not to call him back.

She dropped on the edge of the bed, rubbing the back of her neck.

Being dependent on Colt and Slade was fine for now, but what would happen once she finished testifying? It was a subject she'd instinctively avoided until now.

When this was over, would she ever see her mother, her stepfather and her stepbrothers ever again?

Or would she be forced to start over in a new town, with a new life? The Closed sign on Gifford Furniture made it clear she couldn't return there, even if she wanted to.

The life she had before, the life she couldn't fully remember, was likely gone forever.

Slade kept his voice low, hoping Robyn would get some sleep. "We need to check out the information on the cop you allegedly injured."

Colt raised a brow. "You think he shot himself?"

Slade snorted. "For all we know, one of them shot the other. I mean, it was dark and they were both armed and shooting. Who's to say for sure the cop was hit by a bullet from your weapon?" He paused, then added, "If he was really hit at all."

Colt nodded slowly. "You think it's a ruse to draw us out."

"I do. They have to do something because they've lost us. They have no idea what vehicle we're driving or where we're staying. It's a desperate attempt to get to us, if you ask me. They might figure you'd call into the marshal service or even the police station for info. We could be playing into the hands of those looking for us."

"You may be right," Colt conceded. "But how are we going to check whether or not the story is true? We don't know anything about those two guys."

It was a sticking point. "How about if one of us calls the Greeley police department, pretending to be a reporter? They may give us something."

"The police don't necessarily cooperate with reporters," Colt said.

"Okay, how about this? We call the local newspaper, the *Coloradoan*, find someone who works the crime beat and see if they've heard anything about the shooting?" The more he considered this approach, the better he liked it. "That way, we're an anonymous source. And we may learn something more."

"Do you think they offer a print copy or just an online version?" Colt brought the computer to life and began typing. "I see an online version, but even if they do offer a paper copy, it's not likely to have circulation here in Denver."

"True, but an online version is better than nothing. I'll turn on the news, too." Slade walked over to find the TV remote. After finding a local news station, he sat to watch.

After twenty minutes of searching, they both came up empty.

"What's the name listed in the byline of the crime section?" Slade asked. "Can't hurt to try calling in. Maybe the shooting from last night won't get into the newsfeed until later today."

"Jayne Baldwin," Colt said. "If her picture is anything to go by, she's fairly young."

"And hopefully eager for a story," Slade added. Finding the general number for the newspaper online, he quickly punched in the numbers and waited. "I'd like to speak with Ms. Jayne Baldwin."

"She's on another line, please hold." It was telling that the receptionist who'd answered didn't ask for his name or other personal information.

Thirty seconds later, a female voice said, "This is Jayne Baldwin. Who am I speaking with?"

"I'd rather not say my name, but I was wondering if you were aware of a shoot-out that took place in Greeley last night, around midnight?"

"Shooting?" Her voice sounded surprised. "Where, exactly?"

Slade described the general area, including the dead-end road where the safe house was located and the two cops had shown up. "There were cops involved, so I'm surprised you didn't hear about it on the scanner."

There was a brief silence, and he imagined her

taking notes. Then she said, "I had the scanner on all night. There was nothing about a shooting."

"Check the area out, see if you can find shell casings. I'll call you back later." He disconnected from the call and glanced at Colt. "Nothing about a shooting over the scanner, which is interesting, since they're alleging a cop was shot."

Robyn entered the room in time to hear his exchange with Colt. "Do you think Officer Michaels was one of the cops who shot at us last night?"

He frowned. "We left him cuffed in the hospital room, and the nurse on duty saw what happened, so he should have been taken to jail."

"I didn't read about that in the online edition of the *Coloradoan*, either," Colt said.

Interesting. "Something else to ask the reporter about when I call her back."

Robyn's gaze landed on the television. She went over to sit on the edge of the bed, listening to the local news, which unfortunately had nothing to do with the shooting.

When there was a teaser about the Gifford trial, Slade crossed over and flipped the station. "Sorry, Robyn, you're not supposed to listen to anything about the upcoming trial."

She flushed. "Oh, I guess I forgot." She smiled at her weak joke.

A commercial came on for the University of Denver, encouraging students to enroll today to take the first step toward a new future. She brightened. "Hey, that's where I obtained my MBA with a focus on accounting."

"You sure did," Slade said. These flashes of memories were very encouraging. "You used to tell me you love numbers because they never lie."

"Sounds like something I'd say," Robyn agreed. Then she frowned. "The numbers don't lie," she repeated.

He watched her carefully. "Does that mean something to you?"

She winced and rubbed her temple. "I remember seeing a large spreadsheet and being upset because the numbers weren't adding up. They didn't match what I had elsewhere."

His pulse kicked up. Another memory! Robyn had explained that the inconsistent inventory numbers had been one of the reasons she'd gone down to the warehouse late one night. The night when she'd gotten a glimpse of the guns.

Not just any guns, but AK-47 assault rifles.

"Do you remember who you talked to about that?" Slade asked.

"No." She sighed. "It's like I get these brief fragments that pop into my mind, but they're only one piece of a larger puzzle. But when I go to find the adjacent pieces, they're not there."

He empathized with her frustration and wished there was something he could do to fix it.

Other than kiss her, the way he'd almost done a short while ago.

"It will come," he said instead. "Look how much you've already remembered, and it's only been a day."

"I know I should stay focused on the bright side," Robyn said with a sigh. "Every step, no matter how far, takes me forward."

Personally, Slade thought Robyn was doing exceptionally well under the circumstances. She'd escaped one safe house, suffered a concussion, then was forced to escape a second safe house, dropping into the icy-cold river and floating to a place where they stole a car, and ended up here in this less-than-wonderful motel room.

All without complaining.

He wanted to tell her how strong she was and how much he admired her, but Colt being there made him think twice about uttering his personal views.

Robyn was his witness, nothing more. He knew getting emotionally involved was not only a dumb idea but went against the rules.

"Good afternoon, we have breaking news." The TV show was interrupted by a woman seated behind an anchor desk. Slade moved closer, his gaze riveted on the television. "We have learned about the shocking death of a police officer while in police custody," the anchorwoman said. "Officer Ted

Michaels was being investigated for the attempted murder of a witness. While he was held in a local jail, he was found dead in what may or may not be a suicide. We will bring you more information as this story unfolds."

"Officer Michaels?" Robyn echoed. "The man who came into my hospital room?"

"Yeah." Slade's thoughts whirled. Was this really suicide? Or had Michaels been murdered to prevent him from talking or cutting a deal?

If he'd been murdered, Slade feared Gifford's men were responsible.

And that nothing would stop them from trying to silence Robyn Lowry the same way.

NINE

Goose bumps rippled up Robyn's arms as she realized Officer Michaels was dead.

"I can't believe he killed himself," she said in a low voice. "Just to avoid going to prison."

"I don't think he killed himself at all," Slade said in a curt tone. "I think he was murdered to keep him from talking."

Murdered? She gaped at him. "All this because of Gifford?"

"All of this to get Gifford off the hook from going to jail," Slade clarified.

"I'm going to call Crane, let him know about this." Colt picked up his phone and moved into the other room.

"It just seems so outlandish." Robyn couldn't wrap her mind around it. "Why would anyone do a job for Gifford knowing this is how he treats people when they're no longer of any use to him?"

"All they see is the money, and they always believe they'll find a way to avoid getting caught."

Slade shrugged. "You're right, though, I don't understand it myself. All that time and energy could be used for legitimate work."

"Yes." Robyn repeated the news anchor's statement in her mind.

Officer Ted Michaels was being investigated for the attempted murder of a witness. While he was held in a local jail, he was found dead in what may or may not be a suicide.

Something niggled at the back of her mind. She frowned, trying to bring the memory to the forefront, but it was as elusive as the Christmas star sitting high in the sky out of reach.

Why couldn't she remember?

It was easy enough to recall the coldness of Michaels's eyes when he came into her hospital room, intending to kill her. And how Slade's quick actions had saved her life.

There was something about seeing Michaels in uniform with that awful look on his face that bothered her. She barely knew the man. Why did he hate her so much?

"Robyn? Are you all right?" Slade came over to sit beside her, his green eyes shadowed with concern.

"Yes." She tried to smile but couldn't pull it off. She'd been so excited to remember she'd earned an MBA from the University of Denver, but the news of the potential murder of Officer Michaels greatly overshadowed her brief euphoria. "I just can't believe life means so little to criminals."

"I know." Slade wrapped his arm around her shoulders and squeezed gently. "It's the dark side of human nature that most of us don't experience firsthand."

She glanced up at him; his face was close enough that it wouldn't be at all difficult to kiss him. "But you do, Slade. You and Colt dedicate your life to helping to protect the innocent from the dark side of human nature."

"Yes," he agreed simply. "But you didn't sign up for this, Robyn. You saw something bad and reported it and became a federal witness. Not all people would have done what you did."

She shook her head. "Most people would have." She couldn't imagine not stepping up to do the right thing.

There it was again, the little niggle in the back of her mind that reminded her that some people didn't always do what was right.

Someone she knew? Dale, maybe? No, Dale was harmless.

Then who?

Slade's gaze dropped to her mouth, and she found herself leaning forward, anticipating his kiss. Their lips had barely touched, clung only for a moment when Colt returned.

Slade straightened as if he'd been poked with a cattle prod.

"Crane will try to get the inside scoop on Michaels's death," Colt said.

"That's good. We could use as much intel as possible." Slade's voice was hoarse, and her cheeks warmed as she realized he'd been affected by their brief kiss as much as she had.

"Listen, I know it's bad timing," Colt said. "But is anyone else hungry? There's a restaurant two blocks up the road."

The subject change helped ease the tension between them.

"I could eat," Slade said. "Robyn?"

"Sure." Hearing about cold-blooded murder had put a crimp in her appetite, but Slade's kiss had been a nice diversion. Over too soon, but very nice.

Slade gave her another brief hug before releasing her. She sensed he wanted to say something but didn't.

She rose to her feet. "Are you sure we can't get into my apartment? I'm sure there are family photos there that might help me remember."

"I don't know." Slade frowned, clearly not enthused by her suggestion. "Let's discuss it over lunch."

She nodded and crossed over to where Colt stood with the motel door open. Outside, she could see the family restaurant Colt had mentioned, two blocks up. "Let's walk. I like seeing the cheerful Christmas decorations. This is my favorite holiday."

The men exchanged a glance, likely glad she'd remembered something else, before Slade nodded. "Okay."

They each walked next to her, keeping her positioned safely between them. It was a little awkward; her fingers kept tangling with Slade's, but she tried to ignore the shiver of awareness.

First their brief kiss and now this. What was wrong with her, anyway? This wasn't the time to be thinking about Slade on a personal level.

And why Colt didn't elicit the same response was a puzzle; they were both very good-looking guys.

Maybe her attraction to Slade was her mind's way of dealing with the stress of being in danger and unable to remember anything about her past.

When her memory returned, she might be a different person.

The thought was both intriguing and depressing.

Deep down, she felt certain her feelings toward Slade wouldn't change. But that was her problem, not his.

She focused on the pretty wreaths and glimpses of brightly lit Christmas trees visible through windows. For a moment she remembered another decorated tree, maybe in her church? She frowned, trying to bring it into focus. But it slipped away.

The restaurant wasn't busy. They were escorted to a booth again, much like the one where they'd shared breakfast. The early-morning meal seemed eons ago, instead of five hours.

Once again, Slade scooted in beside her, leaving Colt to take the seat across from them. To distract herself from Slade's nearness, she opened her menu and tried to find something that looked remotely appetizing.

She waited until after they'd ordered their meals before broaching the subject of returning to her apartment again. "You need me to remember everything, don't you?"

"Yes," Colt acknowledged, glancing curiously at Slade.

"I need to get into my apartment and see my family photographs." She paused, then added, "It's really bothering me that I can't remember my mother."

Colt pursed his lips and shrugged at Slade. "Your call."

"I don't like it," Slade muttered. "I'm sure Gifford has someone watching the place."

"I know you said that before, but why would he?" She shifted in her seat to see Slade's face. "I mean, he has no idea I have amnesia, right?"

"Right," Slade agreed slowly.

"So why would he expect me to go back to my place? Did I have any evidence there?"

"No, you turned over the photographs and the spreadsheets to the DA's office." Slade rubbed the back of his neck. "Maybe I should just go get the photographs."

That wasn't at all what Robyn wanted. "But I need to see my apartment for myself. Maybe being in a familiar place will bring more memories to the surface. Being in my apartment along with photos of my family might be all we need to restore my memory."

"Gifford might not know you have amnesia," Slade said, "but he might figure you'd go back at some point to retrieve something."

There was a long silence as the two US marshals considered her idea.

"Your call, Slade," Colt repeated. "I will say she makes a good point. Seeing other familiar things seems to have worked, so why not a quick walk-through of her apartment? *Quick* being the operative word."

There was a pained expression on Slade's face, but then he nodded. "All right, we'll stop by after lunch."

"Great, thank you." She was glad to be taking a step forward in remembering her past but understood there was still a slight risk. "We could go at night if you think that's better."

"I considered that," Slade admitted. "But having a lot of people around during the daytime could be to our advantage. Anyone watching the place might think twice before taking action in front of witnesses."

"Okay." Robyn wasn't about to question Slade's judgment. He was better equipped to make these sorts of decisions.

Their server arrived with their food, and she quickly bowed her head to pray. "Dear Lord, thank You for this food we are about to eat. And please continue watching over us, amen."

When she lifted her head, she was surprised to find Slade and Colt had both bowed their heads for the prayer. It was comforting to be with two men who weren't afraid to pray in public, and she found herself digging into her grilled chicken sandwich with gusto.

Having a purpose while knowing God was watching over you was a wonderful blessing.

"So how do you want to do this?" Colt asked, eyeing Slade over his burger.

"Good question." Slade glanced at her. "I doubt you have a key."

She grimaced. "No, I must not have taken anything with me from the first safe house but the clothes I was wearing."

"Do you remember leaving the safe house?" Slade's question sounded casual, but she knew it wasn't.

"No. But I do remember getting dressed in the hospital. No keys."

"Okay, so Slade will need to pick the lock." Colt grinned. "That shouldn't be difficult."

"Fine, but I think we should park the SUV down the road a spell," Slade pointed out. "I would hate for our vehicle to be compromised."

"Agreed." Colt finished his burger. "Maybe we should pick up the computer and our things from the motel, just in case we need to move to a new location. I'll stay with the SUV while you two go in. If I see anything hinky, I'll let you know."

"Sounds like a plan." Robyn chewed a french fry thoughtfully. "Maybe I can grab a change of clothes while we're there."

"As long as you make it quick," Slade cautioned. "We don't want to be in the apartment any longer than necessary."

"I know." She pushed her plate away, suddenly full. Once Slade paid for their meal in cash, they headed out and walked back to the motel, where they gathered their things as Colt had suggested, to be ready for a quick move if someone followed them. Then they climbed into the SUV.

Their motel wasn't all that far from her two-story apartment building. Colt drove past it and went around the corner to park.

"Ready?" Slade asked.

"Yes." Robyn squelched the flash of nervousness; after all, this was her idea.

One she was convinced would work.

Slade took her hand as they walked casually around the corner, approaching the apartment building. She frowned when she noticed there was a lock on the outside door. She glanced at him. "Are you going to pick that lock, too?"

"The lock doesn't work." To prove his point, Slade pulled the door open.

"Lousy security," she muttered. Inside the building, she instinctively took the stairs to the second floor. "My apartment is 212," she said.

"Glad you remembered." Slade smiled.

Why she could remember something so trivial as her apartment number, but not a picture of her mother or her family, was beyond comprehension.

Her apartment was at the end of the hallway, and her steps slowed as she approached, assailed by a sudden wave of apprehension.

She forced herself to go up and try the door handle, expecting to find it locked.

It wasn't. And worse? She could tell by the scratches around the key opening on the door handle that someone had jimmied the lock to get inside.

"Um, Slade?" She released the handle and stepped back. "It's open."

Gun in hand, Slade pressed her behind him. He pushed the door open and edged inside, sweeping his gaze over the interior. He let out a heavy sigh.

"What?" She peeked around him to see for herself. Her apartment was a total mess—drawers hanging open, contents strewn on the floor, much of it broken. Even her small fake Christmas tree was lying on its side, surrounded by busted ornaments. Stunned, she could only stare in horror. "I—don't understand."

"Stay here, I need to clear the place." Slade's tone was grim. He went farther into the small space, stepping around cushions and other debris as he went from room to room, checking in closets and under the beds. "Okay, you can come inside."

She stepped over the threshold, struggling to keep her emotions in check. She might not have a lot, but what she was left with was mostly junk now. Still, she forced herself to look for family photographs.

There weren't any.

Which wasn't right. She knew in her heart she would have had pictures of her family.

And why the mess? Especially to her tree? Just to be cruel?

Or because they were searching for something?

* * *

Slade quickly called Colt. "Robyn's apartment has been ransacked. We're coming out ASAP. Be ready to pick us up."

"Will do," Colt said, his tone all business.

"Wait," Robyn protested. She was putting things back in their rightful place, a task they really didn't have time for.

"No, we need to get out of here. Colt? Be ready for anything."

"Understood." Colt disconnected from the call.

The hairs on the back of Slade's neck were standing upright, and he wondered exactly when this destruction had taken place.

Shortly after they'd taken Robyn into protective custody? Or recently, as in the past twenty-four hours?

"But—" Robyn abruptly stopped what she was doing, dropping her hands limply to her sides. The stark sadness in her gaze tugged at his heart. As if she hadn't had enough to deal with, now this. He could see she was taking the destruction of her apartment personally.

And he couldn't blame her.

"You're right, there isn't enough time to clean up this mess." There was an edge of bitterness to her tone. "Just—give me a few minutes to grab a change of clothes."

"Hurry." He'd give her two minutes and not a

second longer. He wouldn't rest easy until they were far away from here.

Even the motel seemed too close now. It was time to find a new location.

Why had Gifford's men broken in here? What had they hoped to find?

And if they were looking for something specific, then what was it?

Too many questions without answers.

Robyn emerged from her bedroom with ten seconds to spare. She had clothes and toiletries tucked in a plastic bag. "I'm ready."

Despite his need to get far away, he hesitated. "Did you find the family photos?"

"No." Robyn glanced around the disaster that was once her apartment. "I mean, they could be lying beneath the debris somewhere, but I don't see any broken glass like from a picture frame, do you? Just the broken ornaments."

Now that she mentioned it, he didn't. Moving quickly, he picked up the sofa cushions, some that had been slit open with a knife, and put them back on the couch. Using his foot, he moved things out of the way, searching for anything remotely resembling picture frames.

"Double-check the bedroom, okay? I'll finish in here." Slade took the plastic bag from her hand so she could search unencumbered.

The apartment was small, a single bedroom, so

searching didn't take long. Robyn returned a few minutes later, shaking her head. "Nothing."

That was really strange, but there wasn't time to ponder what the significance of taking family photos might be. Frankly, they were just assuming Robyn had pictures of her family; she hadn't remembered that for a fact.

She hadn't mentioned anything about a family rift, but that didn't mean there wasn't one. Granted, the picture from several years ago that they'd found on social media seemed to indicate she was on good terms with her family. Yet anything could happen over a couple of years.

"Stay behind me," Slade said, leading the way out of the apartment.

Robyn grabbed a fistful of his black jacket, as if needing a physical connection between them. He understood; after all, he felt the same way.

He waited until Robyn closed the apartment door behind them, then they silently made their way down the hallway to the stairs. He wished now that they had chosen to come at night, because he didn't relish the thought of running into any of her neighbors who might want to chat.

The stairs creaked a bit on the way down, something he hadn't noticed earlier. Still, he paused at the bottom of the steps, glancing around to make sure they were alone.

Slade moved toward the apartment door. He

could see Colt driving the SUV slowly down the street, clearly waiting for them.

"We're going to run for it." Slade shifted the bag so that he could take Robyn's hand. He burst out the door, with Robyn right behind him. They dashed toward the SUV. Colt hit the brakes when he saw them.

Slade wrenched open the door and practically pushed Robyn inside. Then he tossed the bag on the floor and slid in beside her. He slammed the door shut.

"Go!" Colt hit the gas. The SUV lurched forward. Seconds later, the rear window shattered into a gazillion pieces.

Someone was shooting at them!

TEN

"Get down!" Robyn reacted instinctively to the gunshot and Slade's hoarse cry. Bending at the waist, she dropped down as far as she could, covered her head with her hands and began to pray.

Keep us safe, Lord!

Colt drove fast, making a series of turns in an effort to get away from the gunman. The sound of police sirens made her feel sick to her stomach. Robyn couldn't see where they were going. She mentally braced for another gunshot, but there was nothing but silence.

Turning her head, she could see Slade had his head down, next to her. His gaze was concerned as he stared at her. "Are you okay?"

She forced herself to breathe, ignoring the cold wind coming in through the shattered window. "Yes. What about you?"

"Fine. But I wasn't the target." Slade reached over to take her hand in his. "Hang in there. Colt will get us out of this mess."

"I know." She trusted these men, especially Slade. But the near miss was still terrifying. "They must have had someone staking out my apartment, just as you feared."

"Yeah." Slade sounded disgusted. "I knew coming here was a bad idea."

"It was my fault for insisting." She pushed away the flash of guilt. "But at least we found out something new. My apartment was ransacked and any photos of my family—assuming I had any—are gone."

"That is unusual," Slade admitted. Then he said in a louder voice, "Colt? Are we clear?"

"Not yet. Hang on," Colt replied. He made several more turns, and she wondered where he was going. Then the vehicle stopped and backed up.

"Where are we?" Robyn peeked up enough to see out her window. "Who lives here?"

"Hopefully, no one is home at the moment," Colt responded. "Stay down."

She lowered her head again, trying to understand his strategy. "Is this sort of like hiding in plain sight?"

"You could say that," Slade said wryly. "Colt, you don't think they got our license plate number?"

"I don't think so," Colt said. But he didn't sound one hundred percent certain.

She swallowed hard. For a long time no one

spoke. Robyn's head began to throb from dangling down between her knees, but she ignored it.

Better painful than dead.

"How long do we have to stay here?" she whispered.

"As long as it takes," Slade whispered back. He reached over to take her hand. "We'll get through this."

Another long period of silence, then the distinctive sound of a car engine. Robyn tensed, praying the owners of the house whose driveway they were parked in weren't arriving home.

"It's a squad car," Colt said in a low whisper.

The police? *Not again, please, not again!* Robyn bit her lip to keep from crying out in despair. Why couldn't they trust the police? Why were they after her, too?

Thirty minutes later, Colt said, "You can sit up now. We're getting out of here."

"I think it's best if Robyn keeps her head down until we're on the highway," Slade said as Colt started the engine. "And the sooner we can get the car window repaired, the better."

"I hear you." Colt drove out of the subdivision, heading for the highway. "First we need to get out of town. I'm glad we stopped by to pick up our things from the motel, since returning there is no longer an option."

Robyn was impressed with the way Slade and Colt were always thinking two steps ahead.

"Any ideas on where to go?" Colt asked.

"I'd hate to be too far from Denver," Slade said with a sigh. "But obviously, Robyn's safety trumps everything else."

"How about Arvada?" The suggestion popped out of her mouth instinctively.

Slade lifted a brow. "You've been there?"

"I think so, yes." She tried to pull the fragmented memory together. The image of a building finally emerged in her mind. "I worked at a clothing store there, in a supervisor position. I clearly remember having to fire an employee for stealing. I think that was my job before I made the move to Gifford Furniture."

"It's good you remember that, but since you have ties to the area, we should go elsewhere," Slade said. "How about Westminster instead?"

"It's fairly flat, not much cover. Maybe Lakewood?" Robyn suggested.

"You remember Westminster and Lakewood, too?" Slade asked.

She shook her head. "Not really. I can picture them in my mind, as if I'd been there or drove through at one point, but I can't remember living there."

Slade nodded slowly. "That's right, too. Okay, Lakewood it is."

"Sounds good." Colt glanced at them using the rearview mirror. "You're both okay back there? I know it's cold."

"Not as bad as the river," Robyn felt compelled to point out.

"I think Robyn's missing family photos are a clue," Slade said thoughtfully. "I know we tried finding more recent pictures of her family, but we should try again."

"Okay," Colt said warily. "But I'm not sure I understand the significance."

"Me, either, but someone went through Robyn's apartment for a reason. Maybe ransacking the place was a way to cover up the fact that they only wanted the photos."

Slade's theory made sense. Especially since Robyn felt certain she would have pictures of her family.

Especially of her mother. It still bothered her that she couldn't remember her mother. They must be close, right? It was difficult to imagine she wouldn't be close to her mother.

Yet she had no way of knowing for sure.

Colt took several smaller highways to reach their new destination. She kept her gaze on the view outside her window, hoping the scenery they passed might spur more memories.

Unfortunately, seeing her demolished apartment

hadn't resulted in a tidal wave of memories crashing upon her the way she'd hoped.

But why? Was it possible she hadn't lived there very long?

And she really didn't understand why they'd ruined her small Christmas tree. Logically, she knew things could be replaced, but the destruction of her tree bothered the most. It seemed—personal.

"Slade, what do you know about my background?" With the wind blowing through the broken window, her hair was flying all over the place, so she put her hand up to keep it off her face to be able to see him. "I mean, did the marshals go back to my college days?"

Slade hesitated, then said, "Yes, we did. You shared an apartment with Angela Percy, your college roommate, until she was married about a year ago. You were her maid of honor at the wedding and moved into the apartment we just left a few days later."

"Angela," she repeated softly. She tried to envision what her college roommate looked like but couldn't. It was so frustrating, she wanted to scream.

"Relax," Slade said. "Try not to stress over this."

She had to bite her tongue to prevent from snapping back. Easy for him to say—he wasn't the one sitting in the fog, wondering when her memory would return and who could possibly want to kill her.

"There's a motel up ahead," Colt said gesturing to the right. "I'll drop you guys off with the computer and the rest of our stuff, then see about getting the SUV window repaired."

Robyn gazed at the motel, trying not to wrinkle her nose at the two-star establishment.

The only good news was that she had a second change of clothes and her personal toiletries. It was more than Slade had, and she felt bad for her earlier annoyance toward him.

Slade was only trying to help. Her memory loss wasn't his fault, and he was doing his best to support her through this.

She blew out a breath and renewed her determination to think positive. To find a way to unlock the memories hidden in the depths of her mind.

Deep down she knew the sooner she managed that, the better off they would all be.

Slade was still reeling at the close call at Robyn's apartment. Repairing the broken window would be easy compared to moving the other obstacles in their way.

Primarily Robyn's amnesia, followed closely by uncovering who within Gifford's team of thugs had ties to the police.

He didn't want to believe the ties were such

that every single municipality was involved, but he didn't want to risk their information being sent over the police scanner.

Thinking of how Officer Michaels had likely been silenced by Gifford's men only added to the need to stay away from all local law enforcement.

No matter what city they were in.

He was tempted to call the reporter again but decided against it. They'd check in on the local news later to see if she'd uncovered anything.

His head ached from lack of sleep, but he ignored it. When Colt pulled up to the motel, he slid out, shaking glass remnants from his clothes and hair.

"Stay here while I check in," he told Robyn, before closing the door. He knocked on Colt's window so he'd roll it down. "Did you use your US Marshal badge on the last place?"

"I did," Colt admitted. "Why?"

"Just wondering."

"They found us at the apartment, not the motel," Colt pointed out.

"Yeah, I know. Still, the whole thing is making me nervous." He shrugged. "How much cash do you have?"

"Plenty" was Colt's reply. His buddy dug in the pocket of his jeans and pulled out a wad of money. "Use what you need to stay off the grid, if that's what we need to do."

"Thanks." He was glad Colt understood. He truly didn't believe Crane or anyone within the US Marshals was leaking information, but the fewer ties to the case and the feds, the better.

At least for now.

It took him a while to convince the middle-aged woman behind the desk to provide two connecting rooms without a credit card, and in the end, he used his badge but only to help her understand his need to pay in cash. The badge was the tipping point, and he soon returned to the SUV with two room keys.

"We're set. Rooms five and six. They're the only connecting rooms in the entire place." He reached in and handed a key to Colt, took the bag from Robyn, then went around to the back to fetch the computer and their things. Thankfully the computer wasn't damaged, and he frowned when he realized there was a hole in the side window, too.

Which meant the bullet had come at them from an angle—the shooter hadn't had a straight shot at them.

He tried to visualize the area, but there were too many possibilities for where the shooter might have been. Still, based on the height of the bullet hole, he didn't think the shooter had been up on a rooftop somewhere.

Not that it mattered at this point. The police were likely crawling all over the area, searching for them. More cops that he couldn't afford to trust.

After brushing away more glass shards, he pulled the computer and their respective bags out and closed the hatch.

A subdued Robyn walked beside him to their adjoining rooms. He used the key to open room five and stepped back so she could enter.

The place was in worse shape than the last one, making him wince. Robyn didn't say anything derogatory about the surroundings as he set her bag on the bed.

"Hopefully we won't have to stay here too long," he said by way of apology.

"It's fine." Her smile didn't quite reach her eyes. "If you don't mind, I need a quick shower to get rid of the glass fragments."

"No problem. I'll see if I can find anything more on the various social media sites and the local news."

"Okay." She took the bag and disappeared into the bathroom.

After tossing his bag on the bed, Slade opened the computer and plugged it in. He scrubbed his hands over his face, trying to ward off the deep desire to take a nap.

They had work to do. He had no clue how long it would take Colt to get the window repaired, but no sense in sitting around and waiting.

He returned to the social media sites, searching for information on Robyn Lowry or her mother, Lucille. Several times, he had to blink and rub his eyes when the pictures grew blurry. After a few minutes, he pushed away from the computer and made a small pot of coffee. They'd need more, but this would work for now.

Then he checked the online newspapers, but found nothing there, either.

He considered calling Crane to fill his boss in on this latest incident, but didn't want to make the call from the motel. Lakewood was only fifteen minutes from Denver, except during rush hour, when the trip would take twice as long. They were close without being too readily accessible, and he didn't want to do anything to compromise their location.

This was their fourth place, which was ridiculous.

Sipping his fresh coffee, Slade went to work searching for anything he could find about Lucille Lowry. He felt certain that finding a picture of Robyn's mother was their best chance in jogging Robyn's memory.

But her mother wasn't on social media at all, and apparently her stepbrothers weren't, either. A little strange in this day and age, but who was he to judge? He didn't use any social media, as his role within the marshal service brought him in contact with a lot of bad guys, and being on any of those sites would be inviting payback in a big way.

Some cops, too, he knew, tended to stay off those sites. Not all of them, but most of the ones he knew.

He thought briefly about how he'd lost Brett Thompson, his witness who had been shot in front of his eyes. And how Duncan O'Hare and Chelsey, had almost been forced into WITSEC because of his failure.

Don't go there, he reminded himself. As much as he'd messed up, things had worked out with Duncan and Chelsey in the end.

Still, losing a witness haunted him, and he couldn't bear the thought of the same thing happening again, so soon after the first time.

Two more search attempts proved fruitless. He sat back for a minute, rubbing his eyes, when Robyn emerged from the bathroom.

She looked even more beautiful, with her blond hair smooth and straight, her desert-brown eyes clear. Waves of a musky perfume wafted toward him, and it took everything he had not to sweep her into his arms for a kiss.

A real kiss. Not the brief one they'd shared earlier.

"I had an idea," Robyn said, crossing over to sit beside him.

"Yeah?" Focusing on a case had never been so difficult. "Like what?"

"Angela," she said. "Why don't we search for my old roommate? There are bound to be photos of me and possibly my family on her site."

"That's a really good idea." Slade knew he should have thought of it himself. He attacked the keyboard with a vengeance and managed to find Angela's social media site without too much trouble.

"I remember Angela's wedding," Robyn said excitedly.

He truly wanted to believe her, but since Angela's site was full of photos from her wedding, he couldn't be sure the memory was real or if the pictures simply looked familiar.

"Do you remember being in college with her?" he asked.

She frowned. "Kind of. I mean, I have a picture of a dorm room in my mind, but it's not very clear."

He nodded and continued scrolling through the photos. "You're in a lot of these, along with Angela's husband, but I don't see anyone who might be your family, do you?"

"May I?" Robyn gestured to the computer.

He turned the device so it was facing her. Robyn was clearly comfortable around computers and the social media sites. After several long moments, she sat back. "I don't think so. At least, none of the other people look familiar to me."

That's what he was afraid of. Robyn wanted to remember so bad, she was imagining herself in these pictures rather than really remembering the situation.

At least, that was his theory. He supposed he could be wrong about that.

"I'm sorry," she said with a sigh. "I was so excited to think Angela might be a good lead."

"It was a very good lead, Robyn. And I told you before, don't apologize for having amnesia." He reached over and drew the computer toward him. "I just had another thought—what if we did a search on Officer Michaels?"

"You think that will help?" Robyn asked doubtfully.

"Let's assume that Michaels knows someone who worked for Gifford. Maybe we'll find a picture of them together." Even though he knew many cops didn't use social media, he was hoping Ted Michaels wasn't one of them.

But he didn't start on social media; he did a search on the guy himself first. It didn't take long for him to find several mentions of Officer Ted Michaels in the *Coloradoan*.

Some were good articles mentioning people he'd arrested, but there was also an article claiming

Michaels was being investigated for use of excessive force.

A picture of Ted Michaels caught his eye; it was obviously taken upon his graduation from the police academy. The article mentioned the graduation date, so he searched for that and pulled up a large photograph of several officers standing together, staring somberly at the camera.

Michaels was in the middle, and he was flanked by two cops on either side.

One of them looked familiar. He frowned and turned the screen toward Robyn. "Do you see Michaels?"

"The guy in the middle," she said. Then her gaze narrowed, and she leaned forward. "Wait a minute, that's Leon standing next to him."

"Leon? Your stepbrother Leon?" Slade asked.

"I remember! Leon!" She reached over and clutched his arm in a tight grip. "I saw Leon outside the safe house before I ran into the church! He's the man who was following me from the first safe house!"

Another piece of the puzzle fell into place. Leon Lowry was a cop and was after Robyn.

Clearly, Leon must be secretly working for Gifford.

ELEVEN

As she stared at Leon's picture, memories cascaded over her. Running from the safe house, pausing near the church, then seeing Leon standing there, wearing all black, gun in hand as he searched for her.

Her stepbrother, a boy she'd watched grow into a man, someone she'd helped care for while growing up, had tried to kill her.

More memories flashed in her mind. Leon working as a cop and part-time as a security guard at Gifford Furniture. Taking weekend shifts when he wasn't working as a cop. At the time, she'd thought it was nice of him to help out on his days off.

Only it hadn't been nice of him. No, Leon was involved in the gunrunning; he must have been assigned to work certain days the shipments were coming in. The way he'd chased her from the safe house proved it.

The realization sat like an elephant on her chest, making it impossible to breathe.

Her mother would be crushed to learn of Leon's involvement in this. Her mother had married George Lowry when Robyn had been about seven years old, and George had two boys, Leon and Joey, who were six and four, respectively. Their blended family had gotten along fairly well, as good as could be expected, and George had formally adopted Robyn.

Why would Leon become involved in this? He was a cop, had dedicated his life to upholding the law.

As had Ted Michaels, she realized grimly.

"Are you okay?" Slade's deep voice penetrated the kaleidoscope of memories.

"No," she admitted honestly. "Leon and I grew up together. I helped care for him and Joey, baby-sitting when our parents went out. I don't understand how he could turn his back on his career and on me." She lifted her tortured gaze to Slade's. "This is going to wreck my mother."

Which, now that she thought about it, might be why she'd self-consciously suppressed the painful memories. Falling down the stairs had caused her mind to go blank, and there was a part of her, deep down, that preferred not knowing the truth.

Ridiculous, as she clearly needed to help put Leon and Gifford behind bars.

"I'm sorry," Slade murmured, putting his arm

around her shoulders. "I'm sure that was a shock to discover your stepbrother is involved."

"Yes." Tears pricked her eyes. "It's so surreal. I never would have thought Leon would do something like this."

On the heels of that thought, another hit hard. The day she caught Leon taking money out of her mom's purse. He'd been sixteen and at the time she'd figured he needed gas money, but when her mother was upset about the missing money, Leon had never come forward, admitting he'd taken it.

She'd covered for him, even back then.

But she couldn't cover for him now.

Was it possible taking money from her mother had been a sign of something deeper? Some strange sense of entitlement?

She wanted to give Leon the benefit of the doubt, after the way he and Joey had lost their mother so young. A few months after their mother had died, George had met her mother. A year later, their parents had gotten married. Robyn had never known her father, who'd abandoned them when she was young, but she could imagine losing a mother would have been traumatic for two young boys.

Battling a wave of despair, Robyn leaned against Slade, reveling in his musky scent. Now that she had her memory back, she realized the feelings she'd had for Dale were nothing like what she felt when she was with Slade.

He listened to her, comforted her, yet also gave her strength to do what was right.

Hero complex? Maybe. She knew the attraction was one-sided.

Although he had kissed her, hadn't he?

As a gesture of kindness and support, not from personal interest. She was a job to Slade, a witness he was tasked with protecting.

A fact she needed to remember.

"What can you tell me about Leon?" Slade asked softly.

She briefly closed her eyes and summoned her strength. Then she sat up and looked him in the eye. "Leon is a cop, but he also worked shifts at Gifford Furniture as a security guard. Looking back, I can see he was probably working shifts when the guns were brought in."

Slade's green eyes were full of compassion. "Do you remember seeing Leon the night you discovered the guns?"

She thought back, bringing that fateful night to the forefront of her mind. "I didn't see him that night. I only saw the other guy, Marcus, and Elan Gifford, too." She swallowed hard. "And Marcus is dead."

"Yes," Slade admitted. "Marcus Rustand was murdered, likely by Gifford or one of his thugs.

Your memory really is back. That was one of the reasons we placed you in protective custody at the safe house."

Her head still ached, but at this point she figured it was more from stress and lack of sleep than concussion related. "I took the pictures and brought them to the police. Must have been one of the good cops, as they quickly got other agencies involved."

"ATF and the US Marshals," Slade agreed. "ATF had been trying to uncover the source of these AK-47s that were showing up across the Midwest, and your photo gave them a huge clue."

Amazing how she'd once taken her memory for granted. Having these images clearly in her mind, along with the inconsistencies in the billing records, was reassuring as far as her ability to testify against Gifford.

Still, learning of Leon's culpability was devastating.

"Robyn, do you have any idea how Leon found you at the safe house in Timnath?" Slade's voice was gentle. "Did you contact your mother?"

"No!" She reared back, staring at him in shock. "You told me I couldn't have any contact with my family, so I didn't!"

"Okay, I just had to ask," Slade said, lifting his hands in a gesture of surrender.

She blew out a breath. Of course he had to ask;

it was a legitimate question. "I won't lie to you, Slade. I very much wanted to talk to my mother, to let her know that I was all right and that she shouldn't worry about me. But I promise you, I did not make the call."

"I believe you." Slade's simple acceptance made her throat swell with emotion.

"Thanks," she managed. "To answer your question, I have no idea how Leon found me. Although we know he and Michaels graduated the academy together. Did the locals know about the US Marshal safe house?"

"No, our protocol isn't to clue in the locals unless absolutely necessary. Which is what I did when you went missing. But up until then, the safe house location should have been incognito."

"Although your boss knew, right?" She remembered how upset Crane had been to hear of their safe houses being compromised. "I'm not saying he's involved, but maybe someone working for him is?"

Slade stared at her for a long moment. "The possibility is one we can't ignore. It's one of the reasons Colt and I have refused to bring you in for a new placement with another marshal."

"They still keep finding me," she muttered wearily. "I guess we know Leon grabbed the pictures from my apartment."

"Maybe, but why would he do that?" Slade's

brow was furrowed. "He couldn't know about your amnesia."

"That's not necessarily true," Robyn said slowly. "Remember the ambulance EMTs? They knew about my amnesia. Could be they mentioned it to Michaels, who in turn told Leon."

"You might be right about that," Slade acknowledged. "Michaels knew you were in the hospital, which is why he came in to try to silence you forever."

"Both of us," she reminded him. "You've become as much of a target as I am."

He opened his mouth to argue, but she put her fingers over his lips. "No, don't say it's your job, Slade. I know that, but you and Colt have gone above and beyond, putting your lives and your reputation on the line to protect me."

He took her hand and kissed it. "Okay, I won't say it, but it's true. This is our job, and you're the innocent victim."

She curled her fingers into a fist, wishing she could hold Slade's kiss inside the palm of her hand forever. Then the sobering reality struck hard. "I'm not going to be able to return to my family once I've finished testifying, am I?"

Slade hesitated, then said, "I'm not sure, Robyn. I won't lie to you. If we can find everyone involved in the gunrunning scheme, then it's a possibility."

"But not likely."

He grimaced. "Let's not focus on the worst-case scenario, okay? We know Leon is involved, as was Michaels. Do you know the names of the other security guards who worked at Gifford?"

She pushed the depressing thought aside to focus on his question. "Now that you mention it, there were several cop friends of Leon's who picked up security guard shifts at the store. I can make a list of names, but I doubt they're all involved."

"Create that list. We'll have someone run backgrounds on each and every one of them."

"Okay." It was good to have something tangible to do. Something that would help bring down the rest of those potentially involved in the gunrunning operation.

But Robyn didn't believe anything they did here would be enough to allow her to return to her life as she once knew it.

And that was the most difficult thing of all to accept.

Slade was relieved Robyn had her memory back, but the anguish on her features made him want to gather her close and kiss her until she smiled.

She typed in a list of five names on the computer. None of the other names were familiar, but he committed them to memory.

Carson Jolly, Chris Temple, Marcus Rustand, Jeremy Stable and Leon Lowry.

Marcus was dead, and he knew about Leon, so that left three other names to put through to his boss.

Not that he planned to call Crane from the motel. He'd have to wait until Colt returned with the SUV.

"I'm missing someone," Robyn said, scowling at the screen. "A new guy, Tony…" She sighed and rubbed her temple. "I guess my memory isn't all the way back to normal."

"Hey, cut yourself some slack," Slade told her. "None of us remembers everything perfectly. Except for those rare occasions of photogenic memories."

"I guess." She didn't look convinced. "I should remember, though, because I seem to remember he came highly recommended from Elan Gifford himself."

The news put this Tony guy up higher on the list. "How often did Gifford do that? Personally recommend employees?"

"Not often," she admitted. "I can only think of two times, when he hired Leon, despite me being his boss, which I felt certain might be a problem, and again with Tony."

"Not Marcus?"

"No, but Marcus was recommended by Leon. They were friends." She frowned. "Or so I thought."

"Okay, so it's highly likely Marcus, Tony and Leon were involved in the gunrunning."

"French," Robyn blurted. "Tony's last name is French. Anthony French." She looked pleased with herself. "Guess I'm ready to testify after all."

"Good job." He planned to check out all the security guards, but having Tony to focus on, along with Leon, was key.

He remembered how brave Chelsey Robards had been about entering WITSEC, and how he, Colt and Duncan had taken down enough of the players so that she ended up not having to go.

If there was a way to do that for Robyn, he intended to find it. Chelsey had already lost her family, but Robyn's mother was out there, wondering about her daughter's safety.

And it pained him to think about the two of them not seeing each other ever again.

His cell phone rang, and since Colt was likely on the other end of the line, he quickly answered it. "Everything okay?"

"Yeah, except that it's going to take another hour before it's finished." Colt sounded disgusted.

"Robyn has her memory back," he told his partner.

"That's great!" Colt exclaimed.

Slade filled him in on her stepbrother's involvement and the shock followed by the fall, likely playing a role in her amnesia.

"As awful as it is for her, this explains the police involvement and Michaels's untimely demise." Colt dropped his voice, making it difficult for him to hear. "Listen, I'm not alone in the waiting room here anymore, so we'll discuss this more when I return."

"Got it." Slade disconnected from the line and thought about their next steps. Since he couldn't call Crane until Colt returned with the SUV, he wondered what he might be able to find out about Tony French and Leon Lowry on his own.

"Slade, why can't we just get the police to arrest Leon and Tony?"

He glanced at her. "I plan to call my boss, but I don't want to do that from the motel, just in case there is someone inside the Denver office helping Gifford out. And while I'd like nothing more than to arrest both of them, all we know for sure is that your stepbrother was following you the night you escaped from the compromised safe house. We can't say for sure he killed Wainwright, the deputy marshal protecting you at the first safe house or that he intended you harm."

"Oh, he intended me harm," Robyn said darkly. "I saw the look in his eye that night. He was angry and determined to find me. And not in a good way."

He understood her perspective, but feelings weren't proof. "I can have my boss bring him in and check his weapon, see if it's a match for the bullet they pulled from Wainwright, but a cop like your stepbrother would know enough to use a different weapon, getting rid of the one associated with the murder."

"Like tossing it in the river," she said dully.

"Exactly." And if Leon had done that, the gun could be anywhere by now.

The fact that Leon had found the safe house at all kept bothering him. Who had known about it? His boss at the marshal office, of course, but Slade couldn't figure any scenario that would have flipped him. James Crane had been with the marshals for well over two decades. He couldn't imagine there was any amount of money that would get him to turn his back on doing what was right.

"I need to start my own list," he said.

"List of what?" Robyn asked.

"Names of people within the Denver US Marshal's office." He glanced at her. "There has to be some way to drill down to find the leak."

Robyn nodded, and he quickly took the computer and made a second column next to her list of security guard names.

"There's a relatively new assistant, Patrice Wilson, and a new second in command to Crane, a guy by the name of Alex Quail."

"If Alex Quail is the second in command, why don't you and Colt report to him directly?"

Robyn's question was a good one. "Technically we do, but Crane is a bit of a micromanager. Since he's always involved, we tend to go straight to him, bypassing Alex."

"I can't imagine Alex likes that."

He shrugged. "He's never complained. Frankly, he doesn't seem to mind as long as things get done." He stared at the screen for a long moment. Most of the office staff were longtime employees, but there was another new guy, Zach Stevens, who had taken a tech role within the organization.

He added Zach's name to the list.

"Three new people from your office and two security guards," Robyn said. "Not very many suspects."

"Should be easy enough to see if there are any connections between the Denver office and Leon," he pointed out. "We already know Tony French is part of this, otherwise why would Gifford bring him in? And you remember seeing Gifford near the box of guns, right?"

"Yes. I remember feeling sick to my stomach at how Gifford was standing over the crate, looking down at the guns with satisfaction."

He nodded, remembering the photograph well. Although the emotion in Gifford's eyes hadn't been easy to see from the angle Robyn had captured.

Still, he would take her word for it. That she'd been that close to a murderer still gave him the chills.

She was smart and savvy, not just from a business perspective, but in her attitude toward life. He admired Robyn, more than he should. Once she'd finished testifying, he'd have no reason to see her again.

He'd have to make sure someone else took on the role of her handler. He was too emotionally invested to keep a professional distance. He was already trying to figure out a way to stay with her through Christmas, her favorite holiday.

Not a good idea, he told himself.

"I just don't understand how Leon could do this." Robyn's whisper drew him from his thoughts. "I mean, buying and selling guns is one thing, horrible enough in its own right, but killing innocent people? After taking an oath to uphold the law? Leon told me once he became a cop to honor his father, George, who was also on the force."

He sensed Robyn was nearing her breaking point. "Try not to dwell on Leon's betrayal. I know it hurts, but he's clearly not the man you thought he was."

"You can say that again," she muttered harshly.

"Robyn, you've given us a couple of leads to go on, which is great. We're going to get to the bottom of this, you'll see."

Robyn abruptly stood and turned away. When she brushed at her eyes, he crossed over to her.

"I'm here for you," he said. "And if you need to cry, I promise I won't melt."

She let out a choked laugh, but then looked up at him. "You're the best thing about all this, Slade. I'm never going to forget you."

Her words punched deep into his gut. And despite his best intentions, he drew her close and kissed her.

Not a brief kiss this time, quickly interrupted by Colt, but a long, drawn-out exploration.

And he knew, in that moment, he wouldn't forget her, either.

TWELVE

Robyn reveled in Slade's kiss, all thoughts and memories instantly wiped away by his embrace. But as much as she wanted nothing more than to continue clinging to him as if her life depended on it, she drew back, ending the kiss. She understood she needed to let him go.

Slade might be her rock during these tumultuous times, but he couldn't be there for her in the long run. His role with the marshals made that impossible. He'd have other jobs, other missions that would take him away from her.

And she had no idea what her own future might hold.

"Do I need to apologize?" Slade asked. "I didn't mean to take advantage of you."

"No," she managed, her voice thick with pent-up emotion. "I've been thinking of kissing you for a long time, since the moment we first met, actually." She smiled and looked up at him. "But we know this—whatever we have between us—can't go anywhere."

Slade's green eyes darkened. "I know there's a lot of uncertainty about what will happen after the trial."

"Yes." There was more to it than that; she'd already failed at one relationship with Dale. A nice guy who'd been bored to tears with her. Slade had no idea how unexciting her day-to-day life really was.

"I'll do my best for you." Slade's promise was low and husky, and she was a little surprised to realize he'd been impacted by their kiss.

Certainly Dale's kiss hadn't sparked this much chemistry or evoked this much emotion.

She would miss Slade, very much. Far more than she'd missed Dale after he'd left.

She pulled her thoughts to more important things. "I know you will, Slade. And I want you to know how much I appreciate everything you've done for me."

He frowned. "I hope you didn't kiss me out of gratitude."

"Not one bit." She tipped her head to the side. "I appreciate Colt's help, too, but trust me when I say I have no interest in kissing him."

A smile bloomed on his face. "Good to know."

Her smile faded as she regarded him thoughtfully. "I imagine your job is such that you travel a lot."

He grimaced. "Yes, I do. I tend to cover Wyoming, Colorado and Arizona, but I have also done a few things in Texas. That's where I'm from, originally."

"I see." She hadn't known he was from Texas. But his traveling reminded her about her mother. About how her mother claimed her father traveled so much that he left his family behind after meeting up with someone else. Robyn had been very young when her parents had divorced, but her mother had made it clear that any man who traveled for his job was not to be trusted.

There was a noise from outside as the room next to the one they were in was entered via a key. Then there was a knock on the connecting door.

"Slade? Robyn? Everything okay?"

Robyn struggled with a keen sense of loss as Slade stepped back and headed over to unlock the connecting door from their side. Knowing more about his job and her lack of a clear future meant there could be nothing between them.

No matter how much she wished otherwise.

"We're fine. SUV has been repaired?" Slade asked. "I thought you said it would take another hour?"

"I decided it was a waste of time to wait, so I arranged for a new ride." Colt shrugged. "Better in the long run anyway, in case the shooter caught the license plate number."

"Good idea, although I think from the angle of the bullet, it wasn't likely," Slade said.

Robyn crossed over to join them. "I shouldn't have insisted on going back to my apartment."

"I think it was good that we did," Colt said. "We know for sure now that Gifford has hired thugs doing his bidding. If we catch one of them in the act, we'll have new charges to pile onto the ones he's already going to trial for."

"We already know Leon is one of them," Robyn said bitterly. "And we've made a list of other possible suspects while you were gone."

"The more information, the better," Colt said with a gleam of satisfaction in his eyes. "Show me what you have."

She and Slade went over to the computer. Slade explained about the possible US Marshal's office employees who might be involved, as well as the security guards.

Colt's expression turned grim. "We need to discuss this with Crane."

"I know." Slade waved a hand. "But I'm not calling him from here. Figured we'd wait until later in the day before we head out for a drive to make the call."

"Patrice Wilson, Alex Quail and Zach Stevens," Colt repeated. "They're all good possibilities, but if we're talking tracking phone calls, I'd lean toward Stevens."

"My thoughts exactly," Slade agreed. "Although Patrice knows firsthand everything Crane has going on, so I don't think we should underestimate her, either."

"Okay, let's start with Patrice." Colt sat in front of the computer and began to search for information. "Good thing Patrice has a very active social media presence."

Standing so close to Slade was distracting. Robyn moved back, reviewing the memories of the case. She remembered meeting with the DA to practice testifying and felt certain she was supposed to meet with him again before the trial.

At least she could remember what she'd seen that fateful night. Her decision to work late had been a fluke, brought on by the inconsistencies in the inventory she'd uncovered.

The fact that Dale had broken things off meant she had nothing better to do but to immerse herself in her job.

Up until that moment she'd seen the guns, she'd enjoyed working for Gifford Furniture, although she'd hoped to move on to a better job in the future. Something that would pay more, so she could save money and invest in a small home or condo.

She sat on the edge of the bed, realizing that her dream of having her own place wasn't likely something she'd be able to accomplish now. Gifford Furniture was closed down, which meant she wasn't getting paid, wasn't able to sock away money for anything, let alone a down payment on her own home.

Besides, how could she put Gifford on her résumé after all this? Being the manager of a store that was nothing more than a front for gunrunning was hardly a point of pride. Even though she'd not been involved with the criminal activity, her name would be associated with it.

Not that it mattered. She felt certain that she'd have to find a new career path once this was over.

Doing what, she had no clue.

"Nothing," Colt said on a sigh. "At least from what I can tell, Patrice doesn't have a connection to any police officers, or any other low-life criminal types."

She glanced over to where the men were both scowling at the computer screen. "Guess that leaves the tech guy, Zach, right?"

"He's next," Colt confirmed.

"When do you want to head out to call Crane?" Slade asked. "Our boss made it clear he expects us to keep him updated on new information, and I'd like to get a BOLO issued for Leon Lowry."

She frowned. "I thought you said my seeing him wasn't enough evidence to arrest him?"

Slade met her gaze. "It's not, but we can still bring him in for questioning as a person of interest."

Remembering the glimpse of hatred she'd caught in Leon's gaze the night she'd hidden in the church made her shiver. There was no denying she'd feel much safer if he was locked up behind bars.

But Leon was smart, and a cop. He'd know enough not to talk without a lawyer, and even if he did, everything he said would likely be a lie.

But it wasn't her call. And maybe turning up the heat would help. She was no expert and nodded slowly. "Whatever you think is best."

"Just give me a minute," Colt said, typing furiously. "Looks like our friend Zach Stevens has a brother who's a cop in Denver."

"Robyn? Will you come and take a look at this guy?" Slade asked. "His name is Tim Stevens."

She stood and went over to look at the picture on the screen. The image was another professional photograph of a nice-looking cop. "I'm sorry, but I don't recognize him."

Colt shrugged, not deterred by this news. "I just think it's interesting as we have other dirty cops involved. And he's got the tech skills to track us if he wanted to."

"Something to keep in mind," Slade agreed. "Let's hit the road. I want to be far from the motel before making the call to our boss."

"Maybe we can stop and get a pizza for dinner on the way back," Colt suggested.

It didn't seem that long ago that they'd had lunch, but glancing at her watch, Robyn was surprised to see that it was near dinnertime.

"You're always about the food, Colt," Slade complained good-naturedly. "Fine, we'll grab something to eat after we talk to Crane."

"Let's go." Colt led the way outside to the new SUV. Robyn followed more slowly, her thoughts bouncing between Leon and her mother. George Lowry, her stepfather, was a cop, so she felt certain her mother was safe.

Would Slade allow her one last moment with her mother before she was whisked away forever? Maybe a small Christmas gathering? Or was that asking too much?

She swallowed hard and silently prayed God would continue to watch over them.

Especially her mother.

Slade waited until they were mere blocks from the downtown office building before calling his boss. It was just after 5:00 p.m., so he was hopeful most of the staff, like Patrice and Zach, were gone for the day.

Although it wasn't unusual for people to stay late, especially when big cases were involved.

Like the pending trial against Elan Gifford.

"Where have you been?" Crane asked in lieu of a greeting. "Do you think I have all day to wait for you to check in? Did you forget your promise to keep me informed?"

Seeking patience, Slade lifted his gaze to the roof of the SUV. "I have not forgotten, and I'm checking in now with an update."

"What kind of update?" Crane asked, his voice rising in agitation.

Considering he'd never told his boss about Robyn's amnesia, he needed to phrase his update carefully. "Robyn hit her head and didn't remember the events immediately preceding her fall until an hour ago. She has identified her stepbrother Leon Lowry as the man who'd followed her after the initial safe house was breached. And you should know," he went on before his boss could interrupt yet again, "Leon worked as a security guard for Gifford Furniture part-time, but his full-time job is that of a Thornton police officer. We also discovered evidence that Leon and Ted Michaels attended the police academy together."

For once, his boss was stunned silent. The guy might be a pain to work with at times, but he was smart and quickly put the pieces together.

"First Leon tried to kill our witness, then Michaels picked up where he left off," Crane mused. "Any other evidence aside from your eyewitness?"

"Not yet." It was a sticking point, he knew.

Especially since Leon was Robyn's stepbrother. The defense could claim Robyn carried a grudge against Leon and that's why she pinned him as being there. Not to mention, Leon could easily claim he was there trying to help his stepsister, not hurt her.

Too bad Leon wasn't in the photograph with Gifford when Robyn had caught him looking down at the machine guns lying in the box labeled "furniture."

"We'll need more to tie him to the crime," Crane said.

"I know, but I think he needs to be brought in for questioning. He's a cop, but even the best cop on the planet can make a mistake."

"Agreed, although we have to assume he'll hear about the BOLO," Crane pointed out.

"If he drops off the radar and refuses to cooperate with an interview, he'll look guilty." Slade almost wished Leon Lowry would go that route. "I'm thinking he's too arrogant for that. He'll come in all innocent and cooperative."

"Yeah, okay. We'll send the word out through the marshals' office. Harder for the locals to ignore a BOLO put out by the feds." There was a note of satisfaction in Crane's tone.

"Thanks." He thought for a moment, then added, "Boss? One more question. How well do you know Patrice Wilson and Zach Stevens?"

Crane grunted. "About as well as I know any of our employees, why? Patrice seems nice enough, never gives me any trouble and keeps things organized around here. Stevens is quiet but gets the job done."

Slade debated how much of his theory to divulge. Crane could be a hothead with all the finesse of a running back barreling through the offensive line. He wouldn't care about how many people he toppled over along the way.

"Here's the thing—every time I call the office, one of Gifford's men manages to find us. I'm not placing blame, or claiming anyone is dirty, but it's a strange coincidence."

Crane was silent for so long, Slade mentally braced himself for another explosion. But when Crane finally responded, his voice was dangerously quiet. "You really think there's a leak in this office?"

He glanced at Colt, who nodded encouragingly. "I don't know, but it's a possibility we can't afford to ignore. Not with two safe houses blown in a matter of hours."

"And you're pointing at these two employees in particular, because…"

"They're relatively new, both employed less than eighteen months, and Stevens in particular would have the skills to track the disposable phone we've been using." Slade was impressed his boss was taking the news so well.

"All government employees are thoroughly vetted before being hired," Crane pointed out.

"I know, sir. Like I said, it's just a possibility I can't afford to ignore."

"Okay, fine. We'll do our due diligence on this side. You keep the witness alive until she has to testify at trial. Understand?"

"Yes, sir." Slade disconnected from the call with relief. "That went better than expected."

"I'll say," Colt agreed. He turned at the next corner. "There's a pizza place up ahead."

"It will be cold by the time we get it to the motel. Let's find something closer to Lakewood," Slade suggested. "On the off chance we are being tracked by Stevens in some way, I don't want to be a sitting duck at a pizza joint."

"Okay," Colt said. "Although we are sitting ducks with the traffic, anyway."

His buddy was right. Slade turned in his seat to glance at Robyn. "I'd feel better if you sat with your head down, and out of view."

She wrinkled her nose in distaste but did as he requested. Once she was leaning to the side, keeping her head low, he glanced at Colt.

"I'd like to talk to Leon when he comes in for questioning, which means you need to stay with Robyn."

"Interesting that you trust me enough to stay with Robyn but not enough to question Leon," Colt said dryly. Slade knew he was kidding, although there was plenty of truth to his statement.

He cared about Robyn more than he'd cared about anyone since losing Marisa.

Which scared him in a way nothing else could.

Marisa had died of leukemia, which was bad enough. She hadn't been a federal witness about to testify against a man who would kill anyone who stood in the way of his freedom.

Hadn't he convinced himself he was better off single? Marriages didn't do well in his line of work, between the long hours, the travel and the inability to talk about what their job entailed. Even Tyler Ryerson, the agent who'd just had a son, had mentioned his wife's dissatisfaction with the job. Adding a baby to the mix wouldn't help matters, and Tyler had mentioned finding a new job to make her happy. Slade had heard from more than one marshal that most spouses couldn't put up with it.

Robyn could.

The minute the thought flashed in his mind, he tossed it out again. Robyn's faith made her stronger than most, but she also deserved to have a nice, quiet life once this was over. A home, a man who would be there for her no matter what.

In this job, the life of a witness always came

first, even before family. Which wasn't a bad thing, when you were talking about innocent witnesses like Robyn.

But there were many witnesses that weren't so innocent. Men and women who were just as guilty but agreed to turn on the higher-ups in the organization in an attempt to avoid jail time.

Getting a new life was often the lesser of two evils.

Easy to understand why the divorce rate among US Marshals was so high.

But not all of their relationships ended in a breakup or divorce. Gully White, one of the older US marshals on staff, had been married to the same woman for twenty years. Gully often referred to Annabelle as the love of his life.

Even after twenty years, there was a light in Gully's eyes when he spoke of Annabelle.

Obviously, there must be a way to make it work. Especially if both parties were equally committed to the relationship.

And maybe, too, if they allowed God to help them through the rough spots.

He remembered the power of Robyn's kiss, then gave himself a mental shake. He was losing it— this wasn't the time to ponder his personal life.

As his boss had pointed out, he had a witness to protect.

The traffic opened up in front of Colt, so he hit

the gas, sending the SUV surging forward. At the exact same moment, a gunshot rang out.

"Get us out of here," Slade said hoarsely, his heart hammering in his chest. "Robyn, stay down, you hear me? Stay down!"

He couldn't tell where the gunshot had come from, but thankfully the SUV hadn't been hit.

At least, not yet.

THIRTEEN

Why does this keep happening? Robyn squeezed her eyes shut and wrestled against the panic washing over her.

She wasn't alone, Slade and Colt were with her, but she couldn't help thinking that one of these times, the bullets aimed at her would find their target.

Silencing her, forever.

She heard Slade giving Colt cues on which way to go. The SUV bucked wildly as Colt went up over curbs to escape.

"Hard right," Slade said curtly. "Through the parking lot."

More rocking from side to side as Colt maneuvered the SUV. There hadn't been any more gunfire, and for a brief moment she wondered if they'd imagined it. Cars backfiring could sound like guns, right?

"Robyn, are you okay?" Slade asked tersely. "I don't think the SUV was hit this time."

"They're getting sloppy," Colt said. "And desperate."

Maybe so, but she couldn't imagine how Gifford's men kept finding her. Unless Slade was right about someone within the marshals' office being involved. She had to admit, phone calls to his boss seemed to be the common denominator.

After another tense ten minutes, Slade said, "I think we lost the shooter."

For how long? Robyn didn't voice the question as she cautiously lifted her head. All the windows were intact, which was a good thing. She found her voice. "Does this mean we need yet another new SUV?"

The two men glanced at each other. "Maybe, but first we need to get back to the motel," Slade said. "Based on the way they keep taking shots at us after we use the phone, I don't think our motel location has been compromised."

A small glimmer of hope flickered. "Staying there until the trial should be fine."

"Only until tomorrow. After that, the federal prosecutor wants you closer to the courthouse," Slade said. "He wants more time to prep you."

"Maybe Tanner can find us something so we don't have to go through our boss and the Denver office," Colt suggested.

"Good idea, I'll call him," Slade agreed.

Robyn understood the prosecutor's desire to

have her close at hand; she was after all his key witness. Still, she dreaded having to face Gifford in the courtroom. The prosecutor had told her to avoid looking at Elan Gifford and to focus only on the two attorneys, him and defense attorney.

But considering she'd worked for Gifford for two years, she knew it would be impossible to ignore him. All this time, she'd thought him a great businessman, when he was nothing but a low-life criminal, making the bulk of his money selling guns.

Not just any guns, but big, ugly assault rifles.

It was disturbing to think of what sort of people bought them and what crimes they'd committed with them.

She shivered and drew in a deep breath. It was important to stay focused. At least Gifford wasn't selling guns or furniture anymore.

By the time they returned to their motel, she was actually hungry. Colt had picked up the promised pizza at a place nearby. It wasn't the best she'd ever eaten, but it wasn't the worst, either.

"Tanner is working on securing a place in Lincoln Park," Slade explained as they ate. "Some friend of a friend is out of town for the next two weeks. Tanner thinks we should be able to use the place for the next few days."

"Long enough for me to testify, right?" she asked.

"Yes." Slade smiled grimly. "We'll keep you safe."

His promise had become more of a mantra, considering all the close calls so far.

When she finished eating, she rose. "I'm going to get some sleep."

"Good idea, for all of us," Slade said. His gaze clung to hers for a long moment. "Good night, Robyn."

"Good night." She went through the connecting door, leaving her side open a few inches, then made use of the toiletries she'd picked up from her wrecked apartment.

Despite her exhaustion, Robyn didn't expect to get much sleep, but the next time she opened her eyes, early-morning sunlight was streaming through the window.

She could hear the low murmur of Colt's and Slade's voices next door. After a quick shower, she went over to join them, inwardly marveling at how much better she felt after a good night's sleep.

"I smell coffee," she said with a smile.

"Help yourself." Slade waved his hand at the coffeepot. "Colt is going to pick up breakfast to go. Just tell him what you'd like."

"I aim to please," Colt drawled, his Texas accent thicker than normal.

She laughed and took a sip of the coffee. "Two eggs over easy with toast, bacon and fruit, please."

Colt nodded and made a note. "All right, I'll

be back in a bit. Try to stay out of trouble while I'm gone."

"We'll do our best," Slade said wryly. He scooted over to make room at the small table for her to join him. "Tanner came through for us. We can use the place in Lincoln Park for the next few days, and there are no ties to the US Marshals' office."

She nodded. "Is it a house or an apartment?"

"A side-by-side duplex, but the owners of the other half also happen to be gone for the holiday so it should be plenty safe," Slade assured her. "And being so close to the courthouse is an added plus. We can make the prosecutor come to us in order to prep you for trial, or we can escort you there and back."

"Sounds reasonable." She was secretly relieved; a duplex would be far better than their current motel room. "I've never met Tanner, but I hope you thank him for me."

"He'll be joining us for the trial," Slade said. "Apparently the judge hasn't received any threats over the past few days and the trial has been postponed so she doesn't want the extra protection detail." He shrugged. "Unless something changes, Tanner will meet us at the duplex later today."

Having a third US marshal intent on protecting her made her feel a bit guilty. Was she worth this much attention? Shouldn't Tanner stay with his assignment of protecting a federal judge?

"It's only for a few days," Slade said softly, as if reading her mind. "Tanner will have another assignment soon, but in the meantime, he wants to help us out. He wasn't happy to hear about the potential leak within the US Marshals' office."

The possibility was sobering. "I guess that means I can thank him in person." She finished her coffee and stood. "I'll make another pot."

She and Slade had made a good dent in the coffee by the time Colt returned with their food. She bowed her head to pray and was surprised when Slade reached over to take her hand.

Curious, she glanced at him, and he smiled and nodded encouragingly.

"Dear Lord, we thank You for this food we are about to eat, and we thank You for keeping us safe from harm. Amen."

"Amen," Slade added. He gently squeezed her hand before releasing her. "It's been a long time since I've attended services, other than the times I protected you, but these past few days have made me realize the importance and the power of prayer."

Colt looked at him curiously. "I didn't realize you'd stopped going to church after Marisa's death."

Marisa? Who was she? Robyn did her best not to look stunned at Colt's comment.

"Yeah, well, it wasn't easy to keep believing in God when a young woman like Marisa dies of leukemia at twenty-nine years old," Slade admitted. "We were supposed to be married, but I had to help plan her funeral instead."

"I'm so sorry for your loss," Robyn murmured.

"Thanks, but I'm better now." Slade's smile was bemused. "Getting shot at tends to put things in perspective."

"It's not the first time and won't be the last," Colt pointed out pragmatically.

Logically, Robyn knew he was right. Slade and Colt both put themselves in danger to protect people like her. The way police officers put their lives on the line to keep people safe.

It was humbling to know that Slade was doing better after losing his fiancée. Maybe her role here was to bring Slade back to his faith.

If so, she was grateful to be given the chance to do that.

Thinking of Slade losing his fiancée made her realize that their kisses probably hadn't meant the same to him as they had to her. He was being kind and supportive, and she shouldn't read anything more into his embrace.

And that was okay—she knew there could be nothing more between them. She forced herself to eat her breakfast, knowing that they had a long day ahead of them, and the trial was looming just three days away.

This nightmare would be over soon enough. She just needed God's strength to help her get through this.

With the added assistance of the US Marshals.

Slade was glad to have Tanner and Colt with him to watch over Robyn. The two men were his closest friends, and he would always trust them to have his back.

What was more concerning was having to bring the prosecutor into the mix. It was a toss-up as to whether it would be better to take Robyn out of the duplex and over to the prosecutor's office to be prepped or bring the prosecutor to their safe location.

He decided to discuss the issue with Colt and Tanner once they were together.

When they finished breakfast, Robyn disappeared into her room to grab her personal items. He and Colt were stuck wearing the same wrinkled clothes, but Tanner had promised to bring new clothes for them.

Thankfully, Colt had gotten replacement weapons when he'd picked up the computer from the main office. They still had their old guns, but after being dunked in the river, accuracy wasn't likely to be one hundred percent.

Fifteen minutes later, they were back in the SUV, Colt behind the wheel and Robyn safely stashed in the back seat.

Despite the bright Christmas lights, the drive back into downtown Denver was tedious. Slade found himself wishing he was back in rural Wyoming or Texas, anywhere other than a large and congested city.

Dark clouds hovered in the air, bringing the threat of snow. He found snow pretty enough, except when it interfered with his job.

"How are we getting into this place?" Colt asked.

"Tanner is going to meet us there with a key," Slade admitted.

Colt groaned. "Tanner is always late," he muttered.

"And you're always hungry," Slade shot back.

"What's your annoying trait, Slade?" Robyn asked. He turned to glance at her, thinking she looked amazing having gotten a decent night's sleep.

"Me? What makes you think I have one?" Slade asked. "Maybe I'm perfect."

"Ha!" Colt busted out laughing. "So not true. How about your inability to let things go?"

Slade knew there was a kernel of truth to Colt's assessment. It had been very difficult for him to move on after Marisa's death. And he also hadn't let go of the way he'd lost Brett Thompson, a witness in Jackson, Wyoming, he'd been assigned to protect, either.

In fact, he tended to ruminate on all his failures. Including nearly losing Robyn twice.

More than twice.

"Maybe you should trust in God's plan," Robyn suggested. "Which I know is easier said than done. I've been struggling with that myself over these past few days. I concentrate on knowing God brought you and Colt into my life for a reason."

It was on the tip of his tongue to point out that God hadn't brought them together, his job had, but he swallowed the urge.

Maybe God did have a plan, but if that was the case, it was a really convoluted one.

His phone rang, but since the number was his boss's, he decided not to answer it. Colt noticed and winced. "Crane won't be happy."

"He'll survive. Tanner is picking up new phones for us, and he's going to get one to Crane, too. Just in case the office has been compromised." Slade resisted the urge to toss his phone out the window. "Crane can wait until then to be updated."

"Could be that they have Leon Lowry in for questioning," Colt said.

His buddy was right, but he wasn't taking a chance. Not when they were this close to their new safe house.

As Colt had predicted, they arrived at the duplex first, without any sign of Tanner. Slade slid out of the vehicle and went over to check things out.

The duplex looked decent from the outside, far better than the motel they'd just left. It would take less than ten minutes to get to the courthouse from here and was close enough that they could also walk if needed.

Tanner didn't show up for almost thirty minutes, but when Colt was about to lambaste him, Tanner lifted his hand. "Hold on. I stopped at the office first to give our boss a new disposable phone to be used only outside the building."

"And that took thirty minutes?" Colt shot back.

"Well, I was maybe a few minutes late before that, and traffic is always a pain." Tanner turned toward Robyn. "I'm Deputy Marshal Tanner Wilcox. It's nice to meet you."

"Nice to meet you, too," Robyn said. "And thank you for what you've already done for me."

"Aw, shucks, it's just part of the job, ma'am," Tanner said with a grin.

"Please call me Robyn. *Ma'am* makes me sound old."

"You have the key?" Slade asked, interrupting them. "It's freezing out here, and looks like it might snow. Get us inside, Tanner, so we can bring you up to speed."

"Ha, speed and Tanner in the same sentence," Colt said. "That's funny."

The smile on Robyn's face as the guys heckled each other made Slade happy. She deserved something to smile about.

The interior of the duplex was just as neat and well maintained as the outside of the building. Tanner made a point of playing tour guide.

"The kitchen, dining area and living room are all on the main level, but there are three bedrooms upstairs. I figure Robyn should take the master to have her own bathroom. You guys can share the other room."

"Why do we have to share?" Colt complained.

"Because I found the place," Tanner said smoothly. "Without me, we'd all be crammed into a couple of lousy motel rooms."

"It doesn't matter who shares, because someone has to be downstairs at all times," Slade pointed out. "We'll be sleeping in shifts as it is."

"I brought groceries and a change of clothes for the both of you—" Tanner looked pointedly at Slade and Colt "—along with the phones. Oh, the boss wants a conference call."

"Of course he does," Slade muttered. "Not that anything has changed from the last time we spoke to him."

"Well, other than the gunfire that somehow managed to miss us," Colt reminded him.

"Gunfire?" Tanner's jovial tone vanished. "What happened?"

"First I need to shower and change," Slade said, taking the bag of clothing from Tanner's hand. "Then we'll bring you up-to-date on what's been happening."

"Tanner, is the judge you were protecting going to be okay?" Robyn asked.

"I hope so." Tanner's voice had an edge to it. "I would have stayed, but that woman is more stubborn than any mule."

Robyn frowned. "You left because of that?"

"No, I left because she told me to get lost and do my job elsewhere," Tanner replied. "The trial has been postponed until after the holidays, anyway." He let out a breath. "Which is fine, because that brought me here, to help you. At least you're willing to accept protection. Some people would rather hide their heads in the sand and pretend the danger will go away."

Slade held up a hand to stop the tirade. "Okay, listen, we need you to forget about the judge."

"Yeah, yeah." Tanner waved a hand. "Go shower and change."

Slade disappeared upstairs to grab first dibs on the bathroom, smiling when he heard Colt ask Tanner, "Did you bring any snacks?"

The shower and change of clothes helped dramatically. Colt took his turn, and soon they were all gathered downstairs around the kitchen table.

Colt had four phones spread out on the table, a new one for each of them.

"You brought them activated and ready to go?" Slade was impressed.

"Makes up for me being late, doesn't it?" Tanner grinned, but then sobered. "Time to call the boss. Here's the number." He rattled it off.

Slade made the call, eyeing everyone around the table. Robyn held her phone like a lifeline, and he had Tanner to thank for making sure she was included.

"Crane," his boss answered curtly.

"It's Slade, and I'm here with Colt, Tanner and Robyn Lowry," he said. "I have you on speaker. We appreciate your willingness to speak to us only through this device and outside the office."

"I've requested a formal investigation into things here," Crane said quietly. "I don't want our office to be the one that causes the marshals to lose our first witness."

"I know." Slade appreciated the pressure his boss must be feeling. Technically, the marshals didn't count Brett Thompson as a loss as the guy hadn't formally entered the program. But as far as Slade was concerned, Brett's death was still his fault. Maybe if he'd tried harder, the guy would still be alive. He forced himself to focus on the present. "What's the latest on Leon? Have you brought him in for questioning?"

"Leon Lowry has called in sick to work and isn't at his home or any of his usual hangouts," Crane said. "Could be nothing, but we're ramping up our efforts to find him."

Slade met Robyn's gaze and knew that Leon's calling in sick was not good news. "Okay, let us know when you find him."

"There's one more problem," Crane continued. "Robyn's mother, Lucille Lowry, hasn't been in to work over the past two days, either. The local authorities have opened a missing persons case on her."

All the blood drained out of Robyn's face.

"Have you tried to contact her?" Slade asked.

"She's not answering her cell," Crane said. "We sent a team to her place, but it's empty, no sign of her."

"Leon has her," Robyn whispered. "I just know it."

Slade was very much afraid she was right. Unfortunately, he had no idea how to find them.

FOURTEEN

Deeply shaken, Robyn knew Leon had her mother and would try to use the woman who'd raised him and his brother, Joey, as a way to get to Robyn.

One thing she didn't understand was where was her stepfather in all of this? Here she'd assumed George would have kept her mother safe.

Had Leon silenced his own father, too?

"Robyn?" Slade's voice brought her out of her thoughts.

"I— We need the police to head over to find my stepfather, George Lowry." She glanced at Slade, then looked at the phone that was still on speaker. "He's still a cop with the Thornton PD. Although he could have retired a few years ago, he's stayed on in a leadership role. I…don't really know what that entails, because I haven't paid much attention since I've been out living on my own since I left for college."

"We can do that," Crane assured her.

"Hold on a minute," Slade protested. "Let's

think this through. If there is a leak within the US Marshals' office, then anything that goes out through normal channels, like our BOLO on Leon, and now this latest news about Lucille Lowry being missing, is out there for the bad guys to hear. I think these guys are one step ahead of us on all of this, because of the information being routed through the main office."

"What's the alternative?" Crane asked testily. "I'm already talking to you guys through some stupid throwaway phone. We need manpower to help us find this guy."

Robyn bit her lip in an attempt to keep her emotions under control. She had an idea, but she didn't want to tell Slade's boss because she knew he wouldn't go for it.

To be honest, Slade, Colt and Tanner wouldn't like it, either.

She captured Slade's gaze, and he seemed to understand she wanted to talk just among themselves, because he told Crane, "We'll come up with a game plan and get back to you."

"Fine." Crane sounded terse, but that may have been because of the inside knowledge that seemed to be leaking from the department.

Slade disconnected from the call. "Okay, Robyn, what are you thinking?"

She nervously wet her lips. "We need to think of a place Leon would use to hold my mom, as a way to draw me out. And then I need to go there and confront him."

Colt and Tanner both raised a brow, but neither one of them said anything, just looked at Slade to take the lead.

"I agree with your first thought on finding where Leon might be hiding, but you're not going anywhere near him," Slade said flatly.

She straightened and narrowed her gaze. "I'm going, Slade. You can go with me or not, your choice."

Slade opened his mouth to argue, but she leaned forward, smacking her hand on the table. "No! Let me be clear, I will save my mom if possible. She has nothing to do with this. It was my choice to testify, not hers. *Mine!*"

There was a long, uncomfortable moment of silence before Colt cleared his throat. "With the three of us backing her up, we might be able to make it work."

"I have a spare gun she can borrow," Tanner added.

She kept her face impassive, although she inwardly recoiled at the idea of carrying a gun.

But she would if doing so meant saving her mother.

Slade abruptly stood, his movements agitated. "Arming Robyn with a gun isn't going to help," he muttered. "Leon is a cop and has who knows how many others helping him. He could easily have three guys with him, outnumbering us."

"We're smarter than he is," Tanner drawled. He turned toward her. "Robyn, do you have an idea of where they might be?"

She sat back, realizing that all of this arguing was moot if they didn't have a clue where to find Leon or her mother. "Leon has his own house, but I'm sure they went there to find him for questioning, right?"

"Yes, but it's not as if they had a search warrant," Colt said thoughtfully. "He could be hiding out in there."

He could, since Leon's house was somewhat isolated from those around him. At the time, she'd wondered how he'd been able to afford the place on a cop's salary.

Now she knew it was guns, not police work, that had paid for the nice home. She cleared her throat. "I would say Leon's house, or maybe the old Gifford building."

Slade stopped pacing and lowered himself into the chair. "Both of those are potential options," he admitted. "But if we assume Leon knows there's a BOLO out on him, I doubt he'll stick around his place."

"Then we start at Gifford Furniture," she said firmly. "Leon would choose something I'd be familiar with, since his goal is to get to me."

Slade wore a pained expression at her statement. "Okay, but Gifford Furniture might be too easy for a savvy cop like Leon. I mean, even the local cops who are not corrupt would think to look for him there. We can check it out, but is there any place else you can think of that might work just as well?"

She automatically shook her head, then hesitated and frowned. "Wait a minute, there's a hunting cabin in Indian Hills that Leon, Joey and my stepfather used on occasion. He could be there."

"Do they own or rent the cabin?" Slade asked.

"I think they rent, but they seem to have easy access to the place." The more she thought about the possibility, the more she liked it. "It's a remote location, and I never once heard anything about their inability to use the cabin when they wanted to. Who knows? It might be open because it's so close to the holiday."

"A cabin that he has access to, but isn't in his name," Slade said slowly. "It's a far better option than Gifford Furniture, and I think that's where we look first."

"Tonight?" Colt and Tanner asked simultaneously.

"Yes," Robyn insisted. "Better for us to sneak up on him in the dark, right?"

There was another long pause before Slade let out a frustrated sigh, pinning her with a hard stare. "We'll go tonight, but you're staying behind me and following orders until we know for sure Leon and your mother are there, understand?"

"Okay," she readily agreed.

Slade scrubbed his hands over his face, then leaned forward. "Robyn, you know there's a chance your mom isn't with Leon at all, and that this is nothing but a trap," he warned.

Her chest tightened painfully, but she refused to think the worst. Her mother was still alive, and they would find her. "I know Leon better than you, Slade. He's tried to kill me several times, without success. Unfortunately, he knows how close I am to my mom. And that means he knows the best and only way to truly get to me is through her."

Besides, she absolutely refused to consider the alternative.

She would know if her mother was dead. Somehow, some way, she'd know.

Slade rubbed the back of his neck. "Tanner, Colt? What do you think? We have the element of surprise if we go tonight."

"Let's do it. If he has Mrs. Lowry and wants to use her as bait, he'll be reaching out to Robyn at some point. Better if we get to him first before he's prepped." Colt jumped to his feet. "It makes me mad when a guy like Leon uses an innocent woman as a pawn in a deadly game."

"I'm in." Tanner rose. "This should be more fun than watching over an ornery judge."

Slade muttered something she couldn't hear beneath his breath, but then nodded.

They spent the rest of the day planning and resting. Once they'd grabbed a quick dinner, Slade was anxious to get to work. "Okay, then let's get ready to hit the road. Robyn, do you know where this cabin is?"

"I do, which is another reason I think Leon picked it. My mom and I went along with them a few times outside hunting season. It was rustic, which my mom didn't appreciate much, but the hiking was gorgeous." She grabbed a piece of paper and began a quick sketch. "Here's the layout of the place," she said as she roughed in rooms.

"And here's the spare weapon I promised," Tanner said, handing her a small handgun. "Do you know how to use it?"

She wrinkled her nose. "My stepdad taught me to shoot a small-caliber rifle, but not a handgun."

Tanner walked her through the basics. "Don't try to shoot at anything far away, but if someone gets close, point at their center mass and shoot."

"I'll try," she said honestly. "I've never hurt a person or an animal, so I'm not sure I have it in me."

Slade scowled. "If some guy is coming at you with a gun, point and shoot. You'll scare him off, even if you miss. And we'll all come running."

She understood these men were all comfortable

with guns, so she nodded. "I promise I'll do my best to follow your advice."

Slade stared at her for a long moment, then said, "I'll drive. You sit up front with me. Once we reach the general vicinity, we'll need to find a place to stop so we can approach on foot."

"Okay." Robyn tucked the gun in the pocket of her hooded sweatshirt and tried to picture the area around the cabin in her mind as they headed out of the safe house to the SUV. They decided to use Tanner's vehicle, since it hadn't been involved in any of the shooting incidents. Tanner tossed Slade the keys, which he caught one-handed.

"Per the GPS, it's roughly a thirty-minute ride, if we can avoid the traffic," Tanner said from the back seat.

"Traffic shouldn't be a problem this late," Colt said. "It's going on seven o'clock."

They fell silent as Slade headed out of Denver. She gave him directions once they passed the city proper. "The cabin is in a wooded area, near the base of the mountain."

"It's nice to have tree cover," Colt said. "Will make it easier for us to approach the place."

"We need to remember that Leon could have several cops there with him, standing guard," Slade said tersely. "There will be nothing easy about this."

Robyn glanced at Slade curiously. His expression was hard and seemed to be etched from stone. She'd never seen him like this.

Then again, they'd never gone to meet a killer before, either.

A killer. She shivered, thinking about the tiny puddle of blood she'd seen beneath the trunk of the sedan before she'd escaped the safe house.

In her heart she knew Leon must have killed Marshal Wainwright, and he may have had something to do with Officer Michaels's death. And he'd obviously tried to kill her multiple times, too.

Had he also killed his friend Marcus Rustand? If his job was to do Gifford's dirty work, then it was highly likely.

The boy she'd read bedtime stories to, had watched after school, helped with his homework… had somehow become this man who would do whatever was necessary to get what he wanted.

It was completely surreal to learn Leon had changed so dramatically. A fact that would hurt her mother even more.

Her mom had to be in the cabin with Leon. She just had to be!

She momentarily closed her eyes and prayed for God to keep her mother safe from harm.

And for the strength to rescue her mother from Leon's greedy clutches.

* * *

Slade didn't like one thing about this little adventure, other than the possibility of getting Leon Lowry into custody.

If he was actually holding Robyn's mother against her will and hadn't already killed her.

At this point, he wouldn't put anything past the guy.

He followed Robyn's directions over the next thirty minutes until she reached over and put a hand on his arm.

"Pull over up ahead," she said. "The cabin is just under two miles from here."

The road was lined with trees on either side, and there were a few small patches of snow. Denver sat at a higher altitude, so it wasn't surprising to see more snow here. He slowed and looked for a spot where he could pull off. When he spied a hollowed-out area, he drove off the road and threw the gearshift into Park.

"Nothing closer?" Colt asked. "It's going to take us time to cover two miles."

Slade smiled grimly. "Robyn's a long-distance runner. I think we can handle a two-mile walk."

"It's a little less than two miles," Robyn said. "But the terrain is rugged away from the road. The cabin is on the right side, and the number on the driveway marker is 308."

Slade nodded. "Okay, let's walk toward the

place and see if there's any sign of Leon or any-one else helping him out. Robyn, I need you to stay behind me at all times."

She looked like she wanted to argue, but she merely nodded, putting her hand over the weapon in her sweatshirt pocket. He wasn't entirely con-vinced she'd do as he'd asked, but for now this was more of a recon expedition rather than a res-cue mission.

Once they knew the lay of the land, and who might be involved, they could come up with a plan to get Lucille out and Leon in cuffs.

One that would have Robyn safely stashed away in the SUV while that happened, if he had his way.

They formed two lines, Slade and Colt taking the lead, with Robyn behind him and Tanner back-ing up Colt. Thankfully they were all wearing dark jackets, which helped them blend in. After going a mile down the road, Robyn tapped his shoulder. "We need to go through the trees here," she whis-pered. "The driveway to the cabin isn't far, and this way we'll be parallel to it."

"Okay." He gestured for Colt to join him in the woods, going in roughly the same direction, for a while until he could see a squat structure up ahead and the glow of a small light shining through one of the windows.

Someone was using the cabin. There was a

truck parked off to the side. "Robyn? Is that Leon's truck?"

"Yes," she whispered.

They'd found Leon.

"Get down," he whispered and dropped to his knees. Robyn crouched behind him, while Colt and Tanner also ducked down, taking cover behind slender tree trunks.

"I saw the light," Colt whispered.

"Yeah, for sure someone is there. You two see if you can get around the back of the cabin," Slade instructed. "We'll stay at the front."

The two marshals nodded and continued making their way silently through the woods.

Slade was surprised they hadn't stumbled upon anyone standing guard, although maybe all Leon's pals were inside the place.

Which could pose a problem.

He drew Robyn close and whispered in her ear, "How big is it inside?"

"Not very," she whispered back. "Just the two bedrooms, a living room and kitchen area. One bathroom. Like I said before, it's rustic. Nothing fancy inside."

"The bedrooms are next to each other, right?" He was trying to refresh his visual of the quick sketch she'd done for them earlier to get a bead on where Leon's pals might be stationed.

"Yes, both on one side," she said. "It's basically

a square, with a living and kitchen area, then the two bedrooms with the bathroom in between."

"And a back door."

"Yes, but not in a direct straight line from the front door," she cautioned. "Oddly enough, the back door is right next to the bedroom, which is off center, as the living area is larger than the two bedrooms."

Thanks to her sketch a picture was coming into more focus in his mind. "Front door leads into the living room, right?" He was glad she'd thought to draw the layout for them earlier.

"Yes."

He nodded slowly. If he were Leon, he'd have Lucille stashed in the bedroom closest to the back door for a quick getaway if needed.

Pulling out his phone, he quickly texted the other two marshals reminders about the interior of the cabin.

If Colt and Tanner could get inside, they'd be able to get to Robyn's mother before he could.

Hopefully getting past the guy likely guarding her without a problem.

Too many ways this could go wrong. The sobering thought made him once again turn to prayer. God may not have saved Marisa from her leukemia, but he hoped and prayed God was watching over them now.

"What's our next move?" Robyn asked.

"I'm going to inch closer, see if I can verify it's Leon inside," he told her. "I need you to wait here, or better yet, go back to the SUV."

"I'll wait." Robyn's stubborn expression was what he'd expected, but he found it frustrating all the same.

Especially since she'd made it clear she wasn't skilled with using a gun.

He hesitated, not thrilled with the idea of leaving her behind. Armed or not, she was vulnerable out here.

Although she knew the area better than he did. At least she'd done some hiking here. Not at night in the dark, but still.

"Stay down," he finally said. "I just want to see if Leon is in there, that's all. This isn't going to be some kind of big showdown. If Leon is inside and we have a good reason to suspect your mother is, too, then we'll make a plan."

"Okay." He wasn't fooled by her easy acquiescence.

He rose and made his way toward the cabin, keeping an eye on the light flickering in the window.

After a hundred yards, he paused and glanced around, searching for a guard.

But all was quiet—no movement, even from wildlife, anywhere.

A shadow moved in front of the window. He held his breath, watching, but the shadow disappeared.

No way of knowing if the shadow was Leon or the cabin owner, taking advantage of a weekend away from the city and coming across a bad situation.

His phone vibrated, and he glanced down to see Colt had sent a group text to him and Robyn.

Woman tied to a chair in bedroom, caught a glimpse of Leon, but no one else so far.

Slade went still as the realization sank deep. Leon was inside the cabin, holding Robyn's mother hostage.

Yet he felt certain Leon wasn't in there alone. And until they knew what they were up against, he wasn't about to risk Robyn or his fellow marshals with a rush approach.

But they needed some way to get Leon's attention.

Like maybe a phone call? He turned to make his way back toward Robyn, a diversion plan forming in his mind.

One that just might work.

FIFTEEN

Leon had her mother.

Colt's text message reverberated in her mind, and in that moment Robyn knew exactly what she had to do. Sending a silent apology to Slade, she tucked the gun in her waistband, nestled in the small of her back, and moved laterally so that she was in line with the front door of the cabin.

Emerging from the trees, she lifted her hands in the air. Ignoring Slade's furious whisper, "What are you doing?" she kept walking.

"Leon, I know you're in there," she called loudly. "You knew I'd find you here at the cabin. I know you have Mom in there, too. I'm the one you want, right?" She shouted louder now, "So come and get me!"

"Robyn, no!" Slade's panicked tone made her wince, but she kept approaching the house. She had to draw Leon out. There was no other choice.

The door opened, and her stepbrother stood

there, dressed in black from head to toe, leveling a gun at her chest.

"It's about time you showed up," Leon said with a sneer. "Now tell those marshals out there to leave or I'll shoot you right where you stand."

Her blood chilled, but she didn't hesitate. "Slade, you and Colt need to back off."

"Get out of here or I'll shoot!" Leon called.

She continued walking toward him, trying to capture his gaze. All the years they'd grown up together in the same house must mean something to him.

It might be the only reason he hadn't already shot her dead. Well, that and the fact that he knew the marshals were hiding in the woods.

"Is Mom okay?" She kept her tone conversational. "There was no reason to drag her into this, Leon. It's me you're upset with, not her."

"Upset?" He let out a horrible laugh. "That's not the word I'd use, sis." Leon stepped back from the doorway, keeping his gun pointed at her chest. "Come inside and see your dear mom for yourself."

It wasn't good that he referred to Lucille as her mom and not his. Was he already distancing himself from the woman who'd raised him like a son so that he could kill them both?

Unfortunately, she was very much afraid that was exactly what Leon intended. The only good thing at this point was that they had an extra marshal that he didn't know about, and she had a gun.

A gun she wasn't sure she could use against Leon.

"Where's Joey? And Dad?" She continued with the small talk as a way to distract him. Her footsteps had slowed as she instinctively did not want to be in the house alone with Leon.

Only she wasn't really alone. Her mother was being held in the bedroom.

"Get inside," Leon growled, his gaze raking the area over her shoulder. "And those marshals better get out of here, or we'll all die here tonight."

He looked dead serious, and she couldn't suppress a shiver. She tried once more. "Slade, Colt, you need to leave! Please? For me?"

In response, Slade came out from his hiding spot behind a cluster of trees. "Okay, Leon, you win. We're leaving." Slade took one step backward, then another, while holding both of his hands in the air. "No reason to do anything rash."

Robyn was relieved yet apprehensive at the same time as she walked closer. One more step and she'd be inside the cabin.

With Leon and, for all she knew, someone else.

A loud bang startled her, and from there things happened in rapid succession. Leon spun toward the sound, Slade shouted at her to get down and she heard the scuffle of people fighting.

To get out of the way, she did as Slade ordered, dropping to the ground. She also reached for her gun again, not at all convinced she could use it.

"Get him!" Leon screamed.

Robyn swallowed hard, her heart hammering in her chest as she realized Leon had backup. Had the guy been hiding in the other bedroom?

The scuffling sounds were louder now, and then she caught a blur as something hit Leon hard in the back. She rolled out of the way in time to see Colt and Leon wrestling on the floor.

Slade quickly joined the fray, helping Colt with Leon, and soon they had Leon disarmed and hand-cuffed.

Robyn pushed to her feet, heading toward the bedroom where her mother was being kept. She almost ran into Tanner, who'd cuffed Leon's helper, a man she didn't recognize. She'd assumed if anyone would be helping it would be Tony French, one of Leon's cop friends they'd identified who'd been hired on as security at Gifford Furniture. But she was wrong. She sent Tanner a grateful look, then hurried into the bedroom.

"Mom? Are you okay?" It broke her heart to see how callously Leon had tied her mother to the chair, a gag around her mouth. Robyn removed the gag first, then went to work on the chair bindings.

"Here, let me," Slade said, joining her. Using a penknife, he easily sliced through the restraints.

"Oh, Robyn," her mother whispered hoarsely. "I was so afraid Leon would shoot you."

She wrapped her arms around her mother's slim shoulders and tried not to cry. "I was worried about you, Mom." She sniffled and hugged her mother close. "Have you really been here two full days?"

"I—I'm not sure," her mother whispered. "What day is it?"

Robyn closed her eyes, battling a wave of fury. "It's Friday night."

"I— Then yes. I think so." Her mother clung to her for a moment, then pushed away. "I need to get up and move. My arms and legs are numb."

Robyn helped her mother stand, holding on to her when she swayed, her knees buckling. Slade offered his assistance, and between the two of them they helped her mom walk into the main room.

Colt and Tanner were speaking in low tones while the two men seated on the floor of the cabin, their wrists cuffed behind them, scowled.

"Slade? We need a moment," Colt said, waving him over.

Robyn took her mother over to the table, far out of Leon and the stranger's reach. Filling a glass with water, she offered it to her mother, who took it gratefully.

Robyn had lots of questions but didn't want

to ask them in front of Leon. Instead, she gently rubbed her mom's upper neck and shoulders in an effort to loosen her muscles.

"Robyn? I need you to stay here with your mom while we get these guys in the SUV," Slade said.

"Okay, but who is the guy with Leon?"

Slade glanced back at them. "According to his ID, his name is Brian Arlo." He turned and held her gaze. "I mean it this time, Robyn. Do not leave here until I get back, okay?"

She glanced at her mom. "It's not like we'd get very far on foot, anyway."

Slade opened his mouth, then closed it again. He turned and walked over to where Leon and Brian Arlo were sitting. Colt and Tanner helped, and soon they had both men upright and headed for the door.

"Gifford will stop you from testifying," Leon abruptly shouted as Slade shoved him forward. "You'll find out what happens to nosy people who don't mind their own business!"

Robyn's jaw dropped, but she quickly regained her composure.

"Shut up, Leon. As a cop you should know that anything you say can and will be used against you in a court of law," Slade said curtly.

"And I've already read these jokers their rights," Colt offered. "Guess the quiet guy is the smarter of the two."

That shut Leon up, which made Robyn extremely thankful.

As soon as the men left, Robyn dropped into a chair next to her mom.

"What did he mean about Gifford stopping you from testifying?" her mother asked.

Robyn filled her mother in on the gunrunning and what she now knew of Leon's role within the criminal enterprise. Then she frowned and asked, "What happened, Mom? How did Leon get to you, and where's Dad?"

Her mother winced and looked away. "I guess I should have told you, things haven't been going well between me and George lately. I—uh, filed for divorce. He's been staying in an apartment, so I was alone when Leon showed up at the house."

"Oh, Mom." Robyn sighed, leaned forward and took her mother's chilled hands in hers. "I'm sorry to hear it, but I wish you'd told me. I would have helped you through this."

"I know," her mother admitted. "I...just hated knowing that I'd failed in two marriages." Her mother's eyes glistened with tears. "I tried so hard, Robyn. I raised those boys like my own and did everything I could to make George happy. But when Leon showed up with a gun, I realized there was nothing I could do to change what festered deep inside."

"I know, Mom. I know." Robyn had never felt

as if her stepfather truly loved her, although he always seemed interested in what she was doing and got along fairly well with Dale. When she and Dale had broken things off, her stepfather had rudely told her she was too plain and boring, echoing Dale's complaints, adding how it was her fault she couldn't hold a man.

Was that attitude what her mother had been up against? Her life hadn't been bad, yet being part of a blended family hadn't always been easy. Robyn had done her best not to cause any problems. To never create any waves. She'd done lots of babysitting for Leon and Joey, making sure never to give George a reason to get mad at her or at her mother.

Yet their so-called family had fallen apart at the seams, regardless of her efforts.

And her mother's.

Robyn wondered if this was God's way of telling her some people shouldn't get married or try to have a family. It didn't work out for everyone.

Like her mother. And her.

The deep feelings she harbored toward Slade weren't healthy if they had no future, and maybe starting over wouldn't be so bad if she could bring her mother with her.

After all, her mother had been threatened by Leon, who was clearly working for Gifford.

She drew in a deep breath and nodded to herself. The trial started Monday, only three days away. The prosecutor's goal was to have the trial wrapped up before Christmas.

After she was finished, she and her mother would be relocated someplace far away from Colorado. Someplace safe.

And she'd never see Slade again.

Slade stepped back as Colt and Tanner gently pushed their prisoners into the back seat of the SUV.

"Leon claims he and his buddy Brian Arlo are the only ones involved," Slade said to Colt. "Should we believe him?"

Colt shrugged. "I don't trust the guy farther than I can throw him, but I'm not sure what he gains by lying. I mean, he did threaten Robyn by saying Gifford would find a way to silence her before the trial."

"I know." And stupid as it was for Leon to have said that, it had bothered Slade to think about the possibility that Gifford had other men working for him, men who were still going to come after Robyn.

Men Leon didn't know personally? Maybe, but maybe not.

Like Colt, he didn't trust the guy.

"Okay, I need you and Tanner to get these guys out of here and to the federal lockup. Get back here as soon as possible, okay? We'll take both Lucille and Robyn to the duplex safe house."

"What about Crane?" Colt asked.

"Call him on the disposable phone once you're away from this area. He won't be happy all this went down without him knowing, but that's too bad. He should be glad to know Lucille and Robyn are safe and that Leon is in custody."

Colt nodded. "Will do. Sit tight. It's going to take a while for us to get these guys in and processed."

"I know." He turned and saw Leon's truck but knew it would need to be processed by the crime scene techs, so using it as a way to get back to the duplex wasn't an option.

Tempting, but he wasn't going to compromise the case against Leon, who right now could be charged with kidnapping Lucille and the attempted murder of Robyn, a federal witness.

They'd wait for Colt and Tanner to return. Slade walked back up to the house, pausing for a moment when he saw Robyn and her mother embracing.

He was glad they'd been able to successfully rescue Lucille. Colt and Tanner had more than done their part. He'd texted them with his plan and that when he used the key word *rash*, they were to move.

His heart had about stopped when Robyn

walked into the clearing in front of the cabin, calling for Leon. At the time he'd been furious, but in hindsight, she'd provided the distraction they'd needed.

Thank goodness Tanner and Colt had been able to breach the cabin through the back.

And that no one had been hurt. Except for Robyn's mother, who'd been tied to a chair and gagged.

Entering the house, he told himself there was no point in yelling at Robyn for not coordinating her plan with him. Especially not in front of her mother.

"I'm sorry, Slade." The first words out of Robyn's mouth surprised him. "You have every right to be angry with me, but I had to confront Leon."

"You didn't have to do any such thing," he argued, despite his decision to let it go. His old tendencies of hanging on to things returned. "You could have trusted that we'd work out a way to free your mom."

"I do trust you, but I was worried Leon would do something drastic." Her deep brown eyes were full of anguish, and he suddenly realized she'd feared Leon might torture her mother, or worse, simply kill her outright.

After all, in Leon's mind, Lucille was just a tool to get to Robyn, nothing more.

How a man could treat the woman who'd raised him so callously was beyond his comprehension. And proved Leon's true and despicable nature. Slade had lost his parents three years ago and still missed them.

If it had been his mother, he might have done something rash, too.

"Never mind," Slade said, waving a hand. "Even though you took ten years off my life, it's over and done. We're going to hang out here to wait for Colt and Tanner to return."

"That's fine," Robyn agreed in a subdued tone. "Thank you."

"You're the one who remembered the cabin," Slade pointed out. "That was the most important thing."

Robyn nodded and sat close to her mother. The poor woman looked like she needed food and sleep, probably in that order.

It took a full ninety minutes for Tanner and Colt to return and another thirty to get back to the duplex. Lucille ate a sandwich they picked up on the way. When he suggested they take her for medical attention after her ordeal, she stubbornly refused, with Robyn backing her up. Slade had to admit he was relieved. He didn't trust that health care personnel wouldn't get word out to local law enforcement, and they couldn't know who was working with Gifford.

When Robyn and Lucille went up to the master suite, he turned toward Tanner and Colt. "Any updates?"

"Crane isn't happy, but we knew that would be the case," Colt said. "Crane mentioned prosecutor Noel Driskol wants to meet with Robyn most of tomorrow and Sunday to prepare for the trial."

"Do we risk taking Robyn to the prosecutor's office over the weekend, when there might be less security?" Slade asked. "Or make Driskol come here?"

"Plenty of risk either way," Tanner drawled. "Personally? I say he comes here, but we meet him a few blocks away to keep from anyone following him."

Slade liked that idea. "Okay, we'll set that up in the morning."

"I'll take first watch," Colt offered. "Tanner can take second watch. You look like you need sleep, Slade."

He wasn't sure he'd sleep much until after Robyn had finished testifying. Something he was looking forward to being done, yet dreading, as he knew it would also end their time together.

He told himself his personal feelings didn't matter, as long as Robyn, and now her mother, were safe.

"Slade?" Colt repeated, snapping him out of his reverie.

"Yeah, I could use some shut-eye." He moved to stand, then hesitated. "What do we know about Brian Arlo, the guy who helped Leon?"

Colt rolled his eyes. "You'll never fall asleep if you keep thinking about the case."

His buddy was right, but he couldn't help the way his mind worked. "I just think we should dig into the guy's background a bit, see if we can connect him to anyone at the US Marshal's office in Denver."

Tanner let out a low whistle. "Good idea, Slade."

"I have them on a rare occasion," he said dryly.

"That's it," Colt muttered. "No one is getting any sleep until we follow this lead. And if I'm going to keep working, I need nourishment."

Colt's grousing made him smile. "Tanner stocked the fridge. Help yourself."

"I bought frozen pizzas," Tanner said. "It's well past midnight—may as well toss one in the oven."

"We had pizza yesterday," Slade protested.

"Pizza is always good," Colt said with satisfaction, looking excited at the possibility of more food.

Slade crowded beside Tanner at the table, craning his neck to see the computer.

Soon the scents of cheese, tomato sauce and pepperoni filled the air.

"Okay, here's Brian Arlo," Tanner said, pulling the guy's police photo onto the screen. "He graduated a year behind Leon Lowry but worked out of the same precinct."

"I don't understand how so many bad cops came out of one graduating class," Colt said.

Slade couldn't help but agree. In the big scheme of things, most cops were good, hardworking, dedicated men and women who joined the force to serve and protect.

A picture caught his eye. "Hey, this woman looks familiar," Slade said, tapping his finger on the screen. The woman in question was standing near Brian Arlo. "Why do I know her?"

Colt and Tanner crowded close. "She kinda looks like Crane's assistant."

"Patrice Wilson," Slade agreed. "She resembles Arlo to the point she could be his sister. But she has a different name, which is also interesting."

Colt's and Tanner's expressions turned grim. Slade kept looking at the woman, wondering if she was the connection to the leak within the marshals' office they'd been searching for.

SIXTEEN

Robyn slept better knowing her mother was here in the safe house with her. The following morning, she tiptoed out of the master bedroom, careful not to disturb her mom, to join Slade and the others downstairs in the kitchen.

She followed the scent of coffee and the sound of the men's voices as they discussed the case.

"Crane is working on getting more intel on her now," Colt was saying.

"On who?" Robyn asked, crossing over to pour herself a cup of coffee.

The men were silent for a moment, then Slade asked, "Are you sure you've never heard the name Brian Arlo before?"

She rolled the name through her mind, grateful to have memories to search through. "No, sorry. He wasn't on the Gifford payroll, if that's what you're asking."

"Your stepbrother never said anything about him?" Tanner pressed.

She frowned at them over the rim of her cup. "No, why?"

"From what we can tell, he was a cop on the force, too. I remembered you mentioning Tony French, but not Brian Arlo." Slade shrugged. "We've been trying to find a connection between Arlo and Patrice Wilson."

It took her a moment to remember Patrice Wilson worked at the US Marshals' office as Crane's administrative assistant. "Why do you think there is one? Although it would explain a lot if she's indeed the leak to Leon."

"Exactly," Slade agreed. He yawned, then took a healthy sip of his coffee. "And the reason we think there's a link is that Patrice Wilson is standing next to him in a photograph, looking enough like Arlo to be a relative of some sort. We worked until two in the morning, then managed to get some sleep. Crane is helping by providing background information on Patrice. If there is a link, we'll find it."

The news was reassuring. First having Leon in custody and now hopefully plugging the leak within the US Marshals' office. At this point, there didn't seem to be much of a threat against her or her mother remaining.

Well, except for Gifford himself, but with the trial starting Monday, she felt certain the risk to her had been appropriately mitigated.

"I'm glad to hear it." She smiled at Slade. "What's on the agenda for today?"

"Prosecutor Noel Driskol wants to spend the day prepping you for trial," Slade admitted. "We're going to arrange for him to come here."

"Okay." It wasn't as if she had much choice in the matter. Besides, her testifying against Gifford was why they were here in the first place, and the main reason Slade and his friends had put their lives on the line to protect her.

It was her turn to do her part in all of this.

She wouldn't fail them now.

"Don't worry, we're going to meet Noel in a neutral location and get him here without being followed," Slade said reassuringly.

"Having Leon behind bars has taken a huge weight off my shoulders," she admitted. "I know Gifford might have others out there, but Leon was clearly the one who kept finding us, especially if it turns out that his accomplice's sister works for your boss."

"Regardless of having Leon arrested, we're not taking any chances." Slade's tone was firm. "Until you've finished testifying, we're going to continue the same heightened level of security."

"I'm very happy to hear that." Her mother's voice caught Robyn's attention. "I had no idea that my daughter was in harm's way over these past few weeks."

The reproach in her mother's brown eyes indicated Lucille wasn't the least bit happy at being kept in the dark about her involvement with the marshal service. "I couldn't say anything, Mom. That was part of the deal when I agreed to go into protective custody."

Her mother's lips thinned, but she simply said, "Well, it makes me feel better knowing there are so many men here protecting you."

"Protecting us," Robyn corrected. "We're in this together from here on out."

"I guess Leon's kidnapping me was good for something, then." Her mother's eyes were shadowed with sadness, and Robyn knew Leon's betrayal had hit hard.

For her, too.

"Are you ladies hungry?" Colt asked, jumping to his feet. "I'm about to make breakfast."

"That's only because you want to eat, right?" Robyn teased.

"Yes, ma'am." Colt grinned. "But I can guarantee I'm a decent cook."

"I'd appreciate breakfast. How about you, Mom?" Robyn asked.

"Yes, thank you." As her mother took a seat at the kitchen table, Robyn poured her a cup of coffee.

The conversation turned to light topics as they ate a few minutes later. Robyn was glad her mother appeared much more relaxed by the time they were finished.

The duplex was nice, but she could have used a bit of Christmas cheer. Not that she was complaining. While she and her mom did the dishes, the guys went to get Noel Driskol, the federal prosecutor.

Prepping for trial wasn't much fun, but Robyn went through question after question, going through everything she'd noticed between the inventory discrepancies and the assault rifles she'd seen in the box labeled "furniture."

Noel Driskol was a decent guy, and he helped her avoid common pitfalls. For example, saying the guns were AK-47s, as that wasn't something she'd known at the time, but a detail that had been provided after the fact.

"Gifford's attorney is going to try to get under your skin during his cross-examination," Noel warned. "He's going to claim you have a personal vendetta against him because he was going to fire you."

"That's a lie," she said hotly.

"I know that, and you know that, but the jury won't," Noel said. "He's going to do whatever he can to discredit your testimony, and I need you to be prepared."

She blew out a breath. "Okay. Let's keep practicing."

They worked all day Saturday and for a few

hours on Sunday before Driskol deemed her ready. "You're going to be great," he told her.

Funny, she didn't feel great; she felt nervous and a bit sick to her stomach. The only good news was that there had been two full days without any attempts to get to her.

Monday morning, Robyn showered, changed into the navy blue slacks and jacket Driskol had suggested she wear to court, and headed down to the kitchen. She was surprised to see Slade already up and dressed. "Morning," she murmured.

"Good morning." He eyed her thoughtfully. "Sleep okay?"

She lifted a shoulder. "Not exactly, but it will all be over soon."

"Not today, though, and maybe not even tomorrow," Slade cautioned. "I know Driskol wants you at the courthouse today, just in case he can call you as a witness after jury selection, but keep in mind that may not happen."

"I know. That's part of the reason I had trouble sleeping." She poured herself coffee and joined him at the table. "After everything that's happened, it seems strange to realize the trial is almost over."

"Very soon," he agreed.

She stared down at her cup for a moment before capturing his gaze. "I'll miss you, Slade."

To her surprise, he reached over to take her

hand. "I'll miss you, too. But you're stuck with me for a few days yet. And we're going to make sure you're safe."

"I know." That wasn't the part that concerned, her. Testifying didn't bother her, either; she was well prepared for what faced her.

What she wasn't prepared for was leaving Slade, forever. She wanted to tell him how much he meant to her, how much he'd helped her just by being so supportive and understanding. She desperately wished he could stay with her a little longer, especially through the holiday. "I couldn't have gotten through this without you."

"You're not giving yourself enough credit," he protested. "You're a strong woman, Robyn. I'm glad I could be part of the team protecting you."

Was it her imagination, or had he emphasized the word *team* on purpose?

As if to prevent her from singling him out from the others?

She wanted to ask, but their brief moment of being alone vanished as Colt staggered into the kitchen.

"Coffee, food," he muttered.

Slade rolled his eyes, and she hid a smile. But her gaze didn't leave Slade. She wanted to imprint his face in her mind.

Foolish, really, as she wasn't the first woman

he'd protected, and she wouldn't be the last. Slade would forget all about her soon enough.

Tanner came in next, then her mother. They ate a quick breakfast while waiting for James Crane to arrive.

When he did step in the house, he immediately filled them in. "I arrested Patrice yesterday," Crane said after introductions had been made. "I found out Brian Arlo is her first cousin. When I confronted her about feeding information to him, she broke down and admitted she'd done that to help pay off her student loan debt." Crane rubbed a hand over his gray hair as he looked at her. "I'm sorry, Robyn. I had no idea that my assistant was leaking information to your stepbrother."

"It's not your fault," she assured him.

Crane turned toward her mother. "And I owe you an apology, too, Mrs. Lowry."

"Not at all," her mother said. "It's my stepson who's involved in this, and he likely talked his friend Brian into helping him, along with your assistant, Patrice." Her mother hesitated, then said, "And I've filed for divorce from George, so no need to call me Mrs. anything. Lucille is fine."

"Thanks for being so gracious," James said.

"Time to hit the road," Slade interjected. "We need to get Robyn to the federal courthouse."

Robyn knew the Alfred A. Arraj Federal Courthouse wasn't far from the duplex, but traffic was always bad, so the sooner they left, the better.

"I'm going with you, Robyn," her mother said. "I want to be there for moral support."

"Oh, that's not a good idea," Slade began, but Crane stepped forward and lifted a hand.

"It's okay, Slade, she can come along. I'll keep Lucille close and protect her as needed."

Slade caught her gaze, and Robyn shrugged. "Fine with me."

They had to take two cars to be seated comfortably. Slade insisted on sitting beside her, while Colt drove their SUV with Tanner riding shotgun. James Crane drove separately with her mother.

Slade kept in communication with his boss as Colt threaded through traffic. She listened as he filled Crane in. "Noel Driskol will be waiting for us at the front of the courthouse. He said we can park temporarily in the no-parking zone, long enough to get Robyn and her mother inside."

"There's a ton of media out front," Colt said. "I can see the mob from here."

"Great," Slade muttered. "Just what we don't need."

"Don't worry, there's a bunch of cops holding the crowd back," Tanner added helpfully. "Nothing to worry about."

She caught a glimpse of the crowd, and her stomach made a nervous somersault. She drew in a deep breath. Slade and the other two marshals were professionals at this kind of thing. She trusted them.

Colt managed to get them past the line of cops to park directly in front of the federal courthouse. She'd driven by the place, but looking at it now, it seemed smaller than she remembered. There was floor-to-ceiling glass along the front of the building, and a long set of stairs leading inside. Red and green lights were trained on the large wreath over the main entrance.

"Ready?" Slade asked in a low voice.

Did she have a choice? She forced a smile. "Yes."

"Let's do this." Slade pushed open his door and got out first, then offered his hand.

She clung to him gratefully, wishing she never had to let him go. The minute she was out of the car, questions peppered her from the crowd.

"Are you nervous about testifying against Elan Gifford?"

"Is it true you're holding a personal grudge against Mr. Gifford?"

"What would you like the world to know about your reasons for testifying here today?"

"Really?" Robyn muttered to Slade.

"Just ignore them," he advised.

She tried to do just that, but it wasn't easy considering they kept repeating the same questions over and over.

Suddenly there was a loud scream, which amazingly shut everyone up.

Robyn turned toward the sound, but then caught a glimpse of a familiar face.

Her stepfather, George, was barely a few feet from her, dressed in a police uniform.

He leered at her and lifted his gun. "No! Gun!" she shouted, belatedly realizing that her stepfather must be involved with Gifford, too.

Just like Leon.

"Robyn!" Slade whirled toward her just as a gunshot rang out.

Robyn tried to keep her gaze focused on George as mass chaos erupted around them. The line of cops surged forward in an attempt to offer protection.

Without realizing one of them was the shooter.

"Robyn, are you okay?" Slade's eyes were wide as he put his arm around her and pulled her close. They were quickly joined by Colt and Tanner, the three of them making a wall around her. "You're not hit, are you?"

"No, but it was George," she gasped. "My stepfather, and he's dressed like a cop."

"Where?" Slade demanded.

"I…lost sight of him, but he was at the two o'clock position," she explained. She craned her neck, trying to see. "He can't have gone far. We need to send the police after him."

"Not now," Slade said.

"Let's get her inside," Colt urged.

"No, wait!" She tightened her grip on Slade, digging in her heels. "Where's my mother? Is she okay?"

"She's with Crane. They're still in the vehicle. I called and instructed them to stay put and crouch down once I heard the gunfire," Tanner explained.

She glanced around and saw that James and her mother were huddled together in the front of the car. She relaxed but instinctively knew it wasn't over.

Not if George Lowry was still out there somewhere.

"Let's go, Robyn," Slade said. "You're a target in the open."

"I know." And her being here was also putting Slade and the others in danger, too. Most of the media people and all the gawkers had scattered, but several of the cameramen were still filming the chaotic scene.

Nausea swirled in her stomach as Slade, Colt and Tanner practically carried her up the stairs and into the building.

"What happened?" Noel asked rushing forward.

"M-my stepfather, George, tried to kill me."

Saying the words out loud only made the situation worse. First Leon and now George.

It was difficult to comprehend how they'd gone from cop to being so far down the criminal path.

"We need to get her inside," Slade said flatly. "I don't like all this glass."

"This way." The prosecutor flashed his credentials at the deputies operating the metal detector and gestured for Slade, Colt and Tanner to take her straight through without stopping until they were in the actual courtroom.

"Sit down, Robyn," Slade said, taking her into the seating area.

She sat, and her entire body began to tremble in the aftermath of what had transpired. Here she'd thought the worst of it was over, that with Leon in jail, there was nothing to be afraid of.

But she'd been wrong.

Why hadn't she considered the possibility of George being involved? Especially after hearing her mother had filed for divorce? He and Leon were similar in a lot of ways, both with an edge to them that hadn't been nearly as apparent while she was growing up as it was now.

And what about Joey? She'd assumed Joey had taken after his mother, as he'd been kinder and gentler than Leon had been. Maybe because as the youngest he didn't have clear memories of the mother he'd lost. Joey hadn't gone into law enforcement the way Leon had but had done training as an EMT.

"We need to get a BOLO out for George Lowry," Slade said. "With a warning that he's not only a cop, but armed and dangerous."

Tanner nodded. "I'll take care of it." He moved away to use his phone.

"Hey, is that blood?" Driskol asked. "Robyn, are you okay?"

Robyn glanced down at her white blouse, frowning when she noticed the streak of red. "I-it's not mine." At least, she didn't think so.

"It's mine," Slade said. "Lowry's bullet nicked me."

"What?" She paled when she saw the jagged wound along the upper part of Slade's left arm. "Why didn't you say something? We need to call an ambulance!"

"No, I'm not leaving you," Slade said firmly.

"Slade, you need to get that wound treated or it will become infected," Colt argued in a reasonable tone. "Besides, we can't have you bleeding all over the courtroom. Tanner and I will watch Robyn."

Slade's gaze clashed with hers, and she forced herself to nod in agreement. "Please, Slade. Get your arm treated. I'll be fine."

Slade blew out a breath, then nodded. "Okay, I'll be back as soon as possible."

He turned and walked away. Robyn swallowed the urge to call out to him.

I love you.

SEVENTEEN

Walking away from Robyn was the most difficult thing he'd ever done. As much as he didn't want to leave her, his arm felt like it was on fire, and he needed to get the wound treated if he was to be of any use.

The sooner he got the stupid thing cleaned up, the sooner he'd be able to return to the courtroom.

He felt certain Robyn was safe, for now. It wasn't as if anyone could shoot at her or stab her while she was in the middle of the courtroom.

Seeing the trail of blood made him wince. He hadn't even noticed he'd been hit at first; his only concern was to keep Robyn safe.

And knowing her stepfather was still out there was not one bit reassuring.

He stopped when he saw his boss escorting Robyn's mother. If he didn't know better, he'd think his divorced boss had some sort of crush on the woman.

"Where are you going?" Crane asked with a frown.

"James, he's bleeding." Lucille stepped forward, her desert-brown eyes, mirror replicas of Robyn's, full of concern. "You've been injured."

"It's nothing, just a scratch," he protested. "Robyn is with Colt, Tanner and Prosecutor Driskol. I'm sure she'll be fine until I return."

"What happened out there?" Crane asked. "I heard the gunfire, but did anyone see the shooter?"

Slade realized his boss didn't know about Lowry's involvement. He glanced at Lucille, not entirely sure she was prepared to hear this.

Yet he didn't think leaving his boss in the dark was the way to go, either. He nodded and cleared his throat. "Robyn recognized the shooter." He turned to Lucille, his gaze sympathetic. "I'm sorry to tell you, but she identified the gunman as your soon-to-be ex-husband, George Lowry."

"Oh, no!" Lucille gasped, covering her mouth with her hand. "That's terrible."

"It's okay, Lucille," Crane said soothingly. Slade hiked an eyebrow at the familiarity between them. "I know it's horrible, but the good news is that no one was seriously hurt."

"Except Slade," Lucille whispered hoarsely. She shook her head in despair. "All these years, I never once considered George capable of this. He's always had an edge to him, one that I did my best to smooth over. But this? Shooting at his stepdaughter? My daughter?" She looked at Crane helplessly.

"I don't understand how he could do it. That he could change this much?"

"I don't know, Lucille," his boss murmured soothingly.

Personally, Slade thought that George's underlying personality had always been along these lines—maybe he'd never gone as far as shooting a gun at his stepdaughter, but most men didn't just wake up one day and decide to turn their backs on the law.

George had likely walked a fine line between cop and criminal throughout the years until greed pushed him all the way over.

But there was no reason for him to spout off about his personal opinions. They'd find out exactly what was going on once they had George Lowry in custody.

"Slade, we need to get George Lowry," Crane said, as if reading his thoughts.

He nodded. "Tanner already put out the BOLO with the warning to consider him armed and dangerous."

"Good," Crane said. "But we need to get locals out there questioning the media folks. One of them might have seen something or even caught the shooting on video."

It was a good point. "I'll make the call before heading to the hospital."

"No, you go get that arm looked at. Get somebody to drive you. I'll make the call, going all the way to the top if I have to." The steely determination in Crane's eyes made Slade grin.

"Okay, you're the boss." He continued walking out through the building, into the crowd that had regathered even after—or maybe because of—the shooting.

Keeping his head down, he returned to the SUV that they'd left in the no-parking zone. He'd get himself to the Denver Health facility, despite Crane's order to get a driver. They couldn't spare anyone right now.

The entire process took much longer than it should have, which annoyed him to no end. The emergency department staff seemed to take their sweet time getting patients through the system. However, he finally was taken back to a cubicle to have his wound cleaned, disinfected and dressed. He'd been provided his first dose of antibiotics through an IV, along with a prescription that he'd filled at the hospital pharmacy.

By the time he drove back to the courthouse, it was already past the lunch hour. He sincerely hoped he didn't miss any of Robyn's testimony, and reminded himself that the jury selection process was tedious and time-consuming.

After he found a regular parking spot and made his way inside, flashing his badge to get through the metal detectors, he was relieved to see that

Robyn was seated outside the courtroom, sand-wiched between Colt and Tanner.

"Still selecting the jury?" Slade asked.

"Yeah." Tanner shook his head. "I don't think they're going to get to Robyn today after all."

"You missed lunch," Colt said. "Plenty of time if you want to grab something."

"I'm fine." He'd munched on chips from the vending machine in the ER waiting room. He eyed Robyn. "How are you holding up?"

"Better now that I know your wound has been cared for," she said with a sigh. "Although I really wish my part in this was over."

"I'm sure." He understood where she was coming from. Having a trial hanging over your head had to feel overwhelming.

At the same time, he knew that once Robyn's part in this was over, she'd be taken away and he'd never see her again.

His heart tightened painfully, but he told himself to ignore it. Robyn had enough to deal with right now; he wasn't going to burden her with his feelings.

Especially since he wasn't exactly sure how to articulate them, anyway.

He cared for her, had begun to fall in love with her. But he'd been down this path before, and it hadn't ended well. Losing Marisa had been hor-rifically painful. No one should have to suffer as she had, only to die regardless of the best medical care the country had to offer.

At the time, he'd asked God why. Why He'd taken such a sweet, innocent soul.

Now he wondered if God's plan was to make sure Slade was here in this place, at this moment, to support Robyn through this particular ordeal.

Another sweet, innocent person who'd done nothing more than investigate a minor inventory discrepancy, only to stumble across a federal criminal enterprise.

"I wish we could wait back at the safe house," Robyn said. "It would be far more comfortable than sitting here in the hallway."

"I know, but Driskol is hoping to begin your testimony today," Slade said. "He mentioned wanting the jury to leave for the day with your words being the last they hear before the morning."

"Trial strategy," Tanner admitted. "It can be very effective."

"Don't mind me," Robyn said, waving her hand. "I'm just tired and cranky. Whatever works best to make sure Gifford goes to jail is a good thing."

"Speaking of jail," Slade said, turning toward Colt. "Any word on George Lowry?"

"Not yet," Colt admitted, glancing at Robyn. "But I'm sure we'll find him."

"I hope so," Robyn murmured.

"Me, too," Slade agreed.

The courtroom door opened, and Noel Driskol poked his head out. "Robyn? Opening statements will be provided to the court right after the midafternoon break. When those are finished, we'll call you up. We should be able to get an hour of testimony completed today."

"Okay." She nodded, but Slade could easily see the flash of apprehension in her eyes.

"How's the jury?" Slade asked.

Driskol shrugged. "Not the best group I've ever tried a case before, but certainly not the worst. Gifford's lawyers are savvy, but we have plenty of evidence. I'm confident things will work out fine."

He disappeared inside, and Robyn turned toward Slade. "Not the best jury? That's not at all encouraging."

"Hey, not to worry. You're going to be great." He forced a smile. "They're going to believe you, Robyn."

She looked down at her hands without saying anything. He eyed his watch, noting that the time was almost 2:15. In his experience, the break would last until 2:30 or 2:40, and then the jury would file in and Driskol would give his opening statement, followed by Gifford's defense attorney doing the same.

Slade was grateful Robyn couldn't listen to whatever defense Gifford's lawyers had come up with. Driskol had warned them that she'd be presented as someone with a grudge against the guy, who'd set him up by faking the photographs to get him in trouble.

He found it hard to believe the jury would buy that theory.

The next hour and forty minutes passed with what seemed like excruciating slowness. Finally the door opened. "Ms. Lowry? You're up."

Robyn let out a long breath and stood. Slade rose, too, and put a reassuring hand on her arm. "Believe in yourself, Robyn," he said in a low voice. "And don't forget, God is watching over you, too."

She smiled, her face lighting up at his words. "Thanks, Slade, I'll remember."

He wanted to pull her into his arms, to protect her from whatever awaited her, but of course, he didn't. Robyn went in first, then he followed, taking a seat in the back row.

Colt and Tanner followed him in, sitting beside him. From his vantage point he had a pretty clear view of Robyn as she stood in the witness box, raised her right hand and solemnly promised to tell the truth.

He noticed she'd buttoned up her jacket to cover the bloodstain. Still, she looked cool and calm under pressure, her expression serious as she looked at Noel Driskol.

His heart swelled with pride. Here was a brave

woman, one who was determined to do the right thing, no matter how many times Gifford's men and those in her own family had tried to stop her.

Even if he never saw Robyn again when this was over, Slade knew he'd never forget her.

Never.

Robyn was glad the box around her seat was high enough that no one in the jury could see how badly her fingers were trembling. She twisted them together and used every ounce of willpower she possessed to look confident.

Despite feeling anything but.

"Ms. Lowry, will you please state your name and occupation for the court?" Driskol asked.

He'd prepared her for this, so she easily responded to his initial basic round of questions. As time went on, she found herself relaxing, the hours of preparation over the weekend paying off.

Thankfully, Noel Driskol made it easy for her to keep her eyes on him, or on the jury, rather than looking at Elan Gifford. Oh, she knew her time before Gifford's attorney was coming, but not today.

And as Slade had pointed out, she had truth, and God, on her side.

Hearing Slade talk about his faith in God had been heartwarming. It made her feel good to know she might have played a role in helping him return to his faith.

His support had been instrumental in all of this. Her gaze found Slade seated in the back of the courtroom. He smiled and gave her a subtle thumbs-up sign.

"Ms. Lowry, please tell the court what happened the night of September 21 of this year."

Noel's question brought her back to the present. As they'd practiced over the weekend, she described how she'd stayed late that Friday night to finish the inventory but had noticed several discrepancies.

After entering her spreadsheet in as evidence, Noel put it up on an overhead projector so the jury could see the various oddities she'd noted.

She heard the softly muttered, "Liar," coming from the defense table.

"Silence," the judge ordered. "Mr. Warren, please tell your client to keep quiet."

"Yes, Your Honor."

Despite her best efforts, Robyn found herself glancing at Gifford. He was staring at her, with a troubled frown on his face, as if he didn't understand why she was sitting here next to the judge and telling lies about him.

A shiver snaked down her spine. Elan Gifford was a good actor. If she didn't know better, she might believe this wounded persona he was displaying in the courtroom.

She glanced over at the twelve members of the

jury and the two alternates. Did any of them believe him?

Robyn forced herself to continue responding to Noel's questions, explaining how the dollar amounts for certain items didn't match what had been documented the year prior. Noel asked more clarifying questions, which she easily answered, but she sensed the jury was losing interest.

It wasn't as if she could blame them. Not everyone was enamored of numbers the way she was. Most people tended to tune out when accounting terms came spewing out of her mouth.

Wasn't this exactly why Dale had called her boring?

A movement near the defense table caught her eye. Elan Gifford leaned forward and murmured something to his attorney, who then jotted a note on his legal tablet.

She looked away, realizing this was exactly what Noel had warned her about. Gifford and his lawyer would try to distract her while she was testifying.

The jury perked up when Noel entered the photographs she'd taken of the assault rifles that same night. Noel made sure to pass several copies out to the jury before putting them up on the screen.

A hush came over the courtroom as everyone stared at the guns lying side by side in the box clearly labeled "furniture."

Noel began asking questions about how she'd happened to take the picture. Once she'd finished explaining how she'd entered the warehouse and heard voices, then followed the sound to where Elan Gifford was standing in front of the open box of guns, she risked another glance at the jury.

This time, she clearly had their attention.

As she shifted her gaze, she saw a man seated directly behind Elan Gifford. He sat with his head down, the dark hair an unnatural color.

There was something about him that bothered her, but she didn't have a clear view of his face. As she continued answering Noel's questions, her gaze returned to the mystery guy wearing what she suspected was a toupee.

The man shifted and lifted his head enough that she could see his features more clearly. A thump of recognition hit hard.

No, it couldn't be.

Could it?

She must be mistaken. Again, Noel's questions pulled her attention from the toupee man, who appeared far younger than you'd expect from someone wearing a wig.

Gifford leaned over to say something to his lawyer, providing a larger gap for her to view the man.

She felt the blood drain from her face. There was no mistaking him.

The man seated behind Gifford wearing the weird black toupee was her stepbrother Joey Lowry.

Her mind raced as she glanced frantically at Slade. What was Joey doing here? He wasn't a cop like Leon or George, but an EMT. Still, he could have played some role in Gifford's gun dealing.

Slade frowned, shaking his head slightly to indicate he didn't understand what she was trying to tell him.

She tried again, looking deliberately at Joey, then at Slade.

He still didn't seem to understand.

"Ms. Lowry?" Noel said.

She dragged her attention back to the prosecutor's question. "I'm sorry, will you please repeat that?"

Noel frowned slightly but went ahead and repeated the question. She responded while trying to figure out whether Joey's presence here in the courtroom was a good thing or something to be concerned about.

Had George sent her youngest brother here? To, what, pick up where George had left off?

No way could Joey get a weapon of any kind through the metal detector.

"Your Honor, I don't have any further questions for this witness," Noel said.

The judge looked at the clock. "Okay, I think we will stop here for the day. Mr. Warren, you may begin your cross-examination of the witness tomorrow morning."

Before they could all rise to their feet, she saw the shiny metal brace around Joey's right knee.

A brace he'd have no reason to wear. Her stepbrother hadn't been injured in any way that she was aware of.

Even as she watched, Joey's right hand pulled something long and thin from the side of the knee brace.

A knife!

EIGHTEEN

Slade frowned as Robyn stared at him, shifted her gaze toward Gifford, then looked at him again. There was alarm and panic in her eyes, and he knew he was missing something, a message of sorts.

But what?

He stood and eased past Colt and Tanner. As he reached the main aisle, he heard Robyn shout, "He has a knife!"

Instantly a man jumped up and thrust his hand toward Gifford. "You ruined my family!"

The courtroom erupted into chaos. The judge began pounding her gavel, calling for the deputies. Elan Gifford slumped over in his chair, a puddle of bright red blood pooling on the white linoleum floor beneath him.

"You ruined my family!" the man wailed again. He stabbed Gifford with the knife again before the deputies reached him. Within seconds they had the man handcuffed and out of the courtroom.

The slim, lethal knife he'd used was lying on the floor where he'd dropped it. Another deputy gingerly picked it up by the end and set it aside to be used as evidence.

Although with this many witnesses, including a judge, and the cameras mounted high in the corners of the ceiling, there wasn't any question of what had happened.

Slade pushed through the crowd, quickly realizing the guy with the knife was Joey Lowry, although the shock of dark hair didn't jive with the photograph he remembered.

He reached Elan Gifford's side as his defense attorney gapped in horror. "Did anyone call 911?" Slade asked, raising his voice to be heard above the din.

"I did! Clear the courtroom," the judge shouted.

"I demand a mistrial," Gifford's lawyer shouted.

By the amount of blood pooling beneath Gifford, Slade knew Joey's knife had nicked an artery, and if they didn't get Gifford some medical care soon, he would die, making the mistrial argument rather superfluous.

"Where's the wound?" Slade asked as he knelt beside Gifford. It was difficult to see with the dark suit he was wearing.

"I can't tell. Appears to be high up on his side," a man next to him answered. Slade didn't know him, but the press pass around his neck indicated he was a reporter.

"We need him off the chair and down on the floor," Slade said. Between the two of them, they managed to get Gifford off the chair and stretched out. He glanced up as Robyn joined them.

"How can I help?" Robyn asked.

It was a testament to her character that she would help the man who'd arranged for several attempts on her life. His, too, for that matter.

Gifford groaned, his face deathly pale. Slade feared if they didn't stop the bleeding soon, it would be too late.

"Help me get this jacket off. We need to apply pressure against the wound," he said to Robyn. Like everyone else, Gifford had been dressed in a nice dark blue suit, crisp white shirt and muted tie.

Only the shirt wasn't white anymore, but saturated with blood. As he ripped it away, he saw the jagged knife wound ran up along the inside of Gifford's left side, all the way up and into the guy's armpit.

He tried to remember his anatomy and physiology. There was an artery up in the armpit, right? The axillary artery? Balling up Gifford's suit coat, he pressed it up and against the wound with as much force as he could muster.

"I can't believe Joey did this," Robyn whispered. "He always wanted to help people, not hurt them."

"I want to know how he got the knife in here." Slade frowned darkly. "Doesn't say much for our metal detector that he brought it through."

"He was wearing a clunky metal knee brace," Robyn informed him. "I think the skinny knife was hidden inside the metal frame. And Joey worked as an EMT, so he knew the right spot to hit an artery."

Slade scowled. The deputies manning the metal detectors should have caught that, but it was too late to worry about it now. "That means Joey had been planning this for a while. He didn't come up with an intricate plan like that, complete with toupee and skinny knife, in a couple of hours."

Robyn nodded slowly. "He claims Gifford ruined our family, but honestly, I didn't realize he was aware of Leon's and George's involvement in all of this."

"George," Slade repeated. He lifted his head and looked for Colt and Tanner. They were standing nearby. "Go find Joey, see if he knows anything about where his father, George Lowry, might be hiding."

The two marshals quickly moved toward the deputies. Moments later, the paramedic unit arrived.

Gifford had stopped moaning, his breathing becoming slow and shallow. Ironically, Slade found himself praying the guy would make it.

Better to rot in jail for the rest of his life than die at Joey Lowry's hand.

The paramedics took over. Slade moved back, his bloody hands dangling at his sides. He watched as the paramedics checked for a pulse and then began CPR.

In that moment he knew Gifford wouldn't make it. No sense in doing CPR when there wasn't enough blood to circulate through his body.

Still, he had to give the paramedics credit. They did CPR, started IVs, gave meds and fluids, packed his wound, then lifted Gifford onto the gurney. With grim expressions they wheeled him out and into the waiting ambulance.

Slade blew out a breath. "Have to say, I didn't see that coming."

"I recognized Joey, despite the toupee he was wearing, and tried to get your attention," Robyn said softly. "But when I saw the knife, I knew what he intended to do." She shrugged. "Maybe if I'd called out sooner, Gifford wouldn't have been stabbed."

"This is hardly your fault, Robyn," Slade told her. "Your job was to testify and to stay focused on the prosecutor. The deputies on duty should have seen the knife before you did." Speaking of which, he looked around to find Noel Driskol speaking in low tones with the judge.

The jury had been removed from the courtroom, and now that Gifford had been taken away, the rest of the courtroom had emptied, as well.

It was over, at least for now. If Gifford survived, he'd have another chance at a trial, but that would take months to arrange.

Besides, he felt certain Defense Attorney Warren might try to work out some sort of deal. Based on the evidence and Robyn's testimony, he'd know the chances of winning at trial were slim to none.

"What now?" Robyn asked.

"Give me a minute to wash up, and I'll get you back to the duplex safe house. You'll need to stay there until we have George in custody."

She nodded, following him out into the now deserted hallway. He didn't want to leave her alone and glanced over in relief when he noticed his boss and Lucille.

"I can't believe Joey stabbed him," Lucille was saying. He thought it interesting how Crane had his arm around Robyn's mother's slim shoulders. The two had certainly bonded over the past few hours.

"It's not your fault," Crane said soothingly.

"Robyn!" Lucille was distracted by seeing her daughter. They quickly hugged, both grieving for the future awaiting Joey.

"Watch over Robyn, will you?" he said to Crane.

His boss nodded, and Slade didn't waste any time. He entered the men's room and cleaned as much of Gifford's blood off him as possible before returning to the hallway.

"I want to see Joey," Lucille was saying to Crane. "It's important I speak to him."

"Maybe later," Crane said, but Lucille wasn't having it.

"Now," she insisted. "Just a few minutes, please, James?"

Slade was surprised when his hard-nosed boss crumpled like a house of cards. "Okay."

Slade caught his boss's arm. "I'm taking Robyn back to the safe house. Bring Lucille when you're finished here. We'll want to keep them both close until George has been apprehended."

"Understood." His boss glanced at Lucille. "Hopefully this won't take long."

His lips twitched, but he didn't say anything more. Instead, Slade escorted Robyn outside to the SUV.

They drove away from the courthouse without any issues. The traffic was still snarly, but he managed to get Robyn to the safe house without further incident.

They both showered and changed out of their bloodstained clothing. He found Robyn in the kitchen cradling a mug of coffee.

"Do you think the judge will call a mistrial?"

He shrugged, taking the seat next to her. "Probably, but try not to stress about it."

"The thought of going through it all again makes me feel sick to my stomach," she admitted.

"I know." He reached over and took her hand. "I'm sorry, Robyn. I should have tried to find Joey before now."

"It's not your fault," she said, offering a sad smile. "And Joey obviously wasn't involved in the gun dealing. Not if he stabbed Gifford for tearing the family apart."

"Still, it was a thread I shouldn't have dropped." Slade couldn't help but wonder if his attraction to Robyn had caused the misstep. "Please forgive me."

"If you forgive me for not reacting to seeing Joey quicker," she countered. She squeezed his hand. "We're human, Slade. Neither of us had any idea Joey would try something like this."

"And succeed," Slade admitted. She was right—if anything, he would have thought Joey was part of the gunrunning, not that he'd stab Gifford, and in the middle of the courtroom, no less.

His phone rang. Still clinging to Robyn's hand, he set the phone on the table with the other and hit the speaker button. "You have information for us, Colt?"

"Yeah, just heard from the hospital. Gifford didn't make it. Apparently, the tip of the knife punctured his artery and his lung, filling the latter with blood. They only did another ten minutes of resuscitation before calling it off."

Robyn bowed her head. He continued holding her hand, offering support. "Did Joey give you anything?"

"Yes, thanks to Lucille, he gave up where George was hiding," Colt admitted. "We sent a couple of squads over. George was found and arrested. And a cop by the name of Anthony French also turned himself in. News of Gifford's death must have gotten out."

That was encouraging news. "Thanks, Colt."

"Gifford's dead," Robyn whispered. "I guess that means no trial."

"Yeah." He tried to gauge her mood. "It's okay to be relieved you won't have to testify again, Robyn."

"Is it?" She lifted her gaze. "I can't be glad a man died today, Slade."

"Not glad," he agreed. He let go of her hand long enough to go around the table and draw her to her feet. "But you're the one who reminded me that God always has a plan. And that's it's not up to us to question His plan."

The corner of her mouth kicked up in a semblance of a smile. "I did say that."

"Robyn, if Gifford had lived, it's likely they would have agreed to some sort of plea deal rather than go to trial again. Especially after how amazing you were on the stand. There's no way the jury would have believed Gifford over you. Not in a million years."

"I'd like to think so," she murmured.

"You might have lost them a bit when talking about your data on the spreadsheet," he teased. "But your pictures of the guns certainly grabbed their attention."

Her smile widened. "I knew I was losing them on the math, but the discrepancy was the reason I went to the warehouse in the first place."

"I know." He pulled her into his arms, pressing a chaste kiss to her temple. "You were amazing, Robyn. Gifford knew it, and so did his attorney. And now that Gifford is dead, and we have George, Tony, Brian and Leon in custody, it's over."

"Over," she murmured, resting her cheek against his chest. "I can't deny being relieved to hear that."

"I mean really over." He leaned back and tipped her chin up to meet her gaze. "You and your mother won't need to go into witness protection."

"We won't?" Hope bloomed in her eyes. "Are you sure about that?"

"Gifford can't hire anyone else to kill you, and there's no reason to do it, anyway." He was glad to be able to give her this. "You and your mother are safe now. We've gotten all the key players. Knowing Leon and George, they'll turn on any other dirty cops in an attempt to get a lesser sentence."

"I…don't know what to say." Robyn gazed up at him. "Except to tell you how much I love you."

He went still, thinking he must not have heard her correctly. "I—uh—" He stumbled over the words. "What did you say?"

Her gaze was gentle. "I love you, Slade. I understand you don't feel the same way, but I wanted you to know. I'll never forget this time we had together. You've been wonderful."

The tightness in his chest eased, and the memories of Marisa faded away. "I'm glad to hear that, because I love you, too."

"Me?" Her desert-brown eyes widened comically. "That's impossible."

That made him laugh. He'd never felt this light, this full of hope. He drew her close and kissed her the way he'd longed to.

Thankfully, Robyn wound her arms around his neck and kissed him back, as if to make sure he understood she felt the same way.

"Will you spend Christmas with me?" Robyn asked softly.

"Absolutely," he whispered, capturing her mouth in another kiss.

"Well, don't let us interrupt," a voice drawled from the doorway.

He'd had been so lost in their kiss, he hadn't heard Crane and Lucille come in.

"I love your daughter, Ms. Lowry," Slade declared, feeling downright light-headed from the impact of Robyn's kiss.

"And I love, Slade, too," Robyn said, her cheeks adorably pink with embarrassment.

"That makes me very happy," Lucille said, although Slade thought there was a shadow of doubt in her eyes.

"But?" he said, putting his arm around Robyn's shoulders to keep her anchored to his side. If he had his way, he wouldn't let go of her for a long time.

If ever.

"I…heard there's a lot of travel involved in being a US Marshal," Lucille finally admitted. "Being apart for long periods of time makes having a relationship difficult."

"Mom, Slade is not my father," Robyn said firmly. "He would never leave a wife and daughter behind to start a new family elsewhere."

"I know," Lucille protested, although clearly she didn't quite believe it.

"I've already considered the travel aspect of my job as being a potential problem," Slade admitted. "I have options. I can ask for a permanent relocation to the Denver office, right, boss?"

"Right," Crane admitted.

"Wait a minute," Robyn protested. She looked at him with exasperation. "I would never ask you to change your job for me. Being a US deputy marshal is who you are, Slade. I'm proud of the work you do."

Her comment made him want to kiss her again. And again, and again. "I know you would never ask such a thing, but I would be taking a job change for both of us, Robyn." He hesitated, then added, "When my fiancée died two years ago, I was too late to see her before she was gone. I won't make that mistake again."

"I…didn't know," Robyn said quietly. "That must have been very difficult."

"Yes, but that's in the past." He'd always care for Marisa, but he loved Robyn. Loved her grittiness and determination to do what was right. She was loyal and brave yet sweet and kind.

He even loved how she tried to make spreadsheets interesting.

"I'm focused on the future," he said softly. "After all, God brought us together for a reason, right?"

"Right," she agreed.

He kissed her again, ignoring the bemused expressions on Lucille's and Crane's faces.

"Whoa, what's this?" Colt asked as he came into the safehouse followed by Tanner.

Slade broke off the kiss with a sigh. "What does it look like?" he asked testily.

"No reason to get cranky," Tanner said with a wide grin. "We've been wondering when you'd get around to kissing Robyn, that's all."

"Some friends you are," he groused.

"I think you have wonderful friends," Robyn defended. Then she frowned. "Although why on earth would you wonder when we'd kiss?"

Colt shook his head. "If you had any idea how the two of you looked at each other when you thought the other wasn't looking, you wouldn't need to ask that question."

"Okay, okay." Slade held up his hand. "We get the picture."

"I'm hungry," Colt announced.

Slade couldn't help but laugh. "Of course you are."

"I'll make dinner," Lucille offered.

"I can help," Colt said.

Slade drew Robyn aside, away from the group in the kitchen. "I love you, Robyn."

"I love you, too." She kissed him again.

And he knew in that moment how much he looked forward to being a part of a family.

Not one by blood, but through friendship.

And love.

EPILOGUE

Christmas Eve

Robyn opened her apartment door to find Slade standing there with a wide grin on his face. "Merry Christmas," she greeted him warmly. "Come on in."

"Merry Christmas to you, too."

She opened the door wider to let him inside. Tomorrow her mother was making a Christmas luncheon, but tonight was just for the two of them.

Slade had helped her clean up the apartment, going as far as to buy a new and bigger Christmas tree to replace her small broken one. They couldn't have real trees in the apartment for fire reasons, but the one he'd chosen for her was beautiful.

The past week had been full of change. Somehow, despite being so close to the holiday, she'd landed a new job with an actual accounting firm.

She didn't start until after the first of the year, but she was thrilled with the salary they'd offered her.

Slade was also transitioning into a new role within the Denver US Marshals' office in the new year, too.

As Slade had predicted, her stepfather and stepbrother had both provided additional information on those involved in the gun dealing to receive lighter sentences. She was horrified to realize there had been two additional dirty cops in the Thornton police force, Tony French being one of them, along with another guy she hadn't known.

The only good news was that her stepfather didn't contest the divorce, and her mother had already put her current house on the market, hoping to purchase something much smaller.

And even more interesting was the fact that James Crane had visited twice already and was planning to attend their Christmas luncheon.

"I've made spaghetti. It'll be ready in about twenty minutes." Robyn couldn't deny feeling nervous. She wasn't exactly the best cook on the planet. Good thing she hadn't fallen for Colt; the poor man would starve.

"Smells delicious." Slade held out his hand. "Come sit by the tree with me."

She took his hand and followed him to the sofa.

To her utter and complete surprise, he went down on one knee and held out a small velvet box.

"What is this?" Her voice was breathless.

"Robyn, I love you and want to marry you. I know it's very soon, but I feel as if I've known you for months instead of weeks. And if you don't like this ring, we'll get something different. Will you please marry me?" He opened the box, revealing a sparkling diamond engagement ring.

"Oh, Slade." Her eyes filled with tears, and she nodded. She held out her left hand so he could slide the ring on, unsurprised it fit perfectly. "Yes, of course I'll marry you."

"I love you," he repeated, then stood and pulled her into his arms.

His kiss made her head swim, but then suddenly she pulled back, gaping at him. "Wait a minute. I don't have nearly as expensive of a gift for you."

He threw his head back and laughed. "Oh, Robyn. You agreeing to be my wife is the only gift I need."

Flushing, she broke out of his embrace and picked up a small wrapped box from beneath the tree. "For you."

Slade eyed her curiously as he carefully unwrapped the gift. When he opened the box, he smiled. "It's a picture ornament of us."

"Yes. Our first Christmas together." She

watched with amazement as he hung it on the closest tree branch.

"It's perfect, Robyn. Just like you." He pulled her close for another kiss.

Robyn kissed Slade back, thinking she'd never been so happy.

Or so blessed.

* * * * *

If you enjoyed this book,
don't miss these other stories
from Laura Scott:

Shielding His Christmas Witness
The Only Witness
Christmas Amnesia
Shattered Lullaby
Primary Suspect
Protecting His Secret Son
Soldier's Christmas Secrets
Guarded by the Soldier
Wyoming Mountain Escape

Available now from Love Inspired Suspense!

Find more great reads at
www.LoveInspired.com

Dear Reader,

I hope you enjoyed reading Slade and Robyn's story! I knew when I introduced Slade Brooks, Colt Nelson and Tanner Wilcox in *Wyoming Mountain Escape* that these three heroes deserved stories of their own. I can't wait to start working on the next story.

I'm very blessed to have wonderful readers! Please don't hesitate to drop me a note, either through my website, www.laurascottbooks.com, via Facebook at https://www.Facebook.com/Laura-ScottBooks and on Twitter https://Twitter.com/laurascottbooks. I always respond to notes from my fans.

Please take a moment to sign up for my monthly newsletter through my website. This is where I reveal new covers and book release news. All subscribers receive a free Crystal Lake novella that is not available for purchase at any store.

Until next time,
Laura Scott

Get 4 FREE REWARDS!

We'll send you 2 FREE Books plus 2 FREE Mystery Gifts.

Harlequin Heartwarming Larger-Print books will connect you to uplifting stories where the bonds of friendship, family and community unite.

FREE
Value Over
$20

HARLEQUIN SELECTS COLLECTION

19 FREE BOOKS IN ALL!

From Robyn Carr to RaeAnne Thayne to
Linda Lael Miller and Sherryl Woods we promise
(actually, GUARANTEE!) each author in the
Harlequin Selects collection has seen their name on
the *New York Times* or *USA TODAY* bestseller lists!

YES! Please send me the **Harlequin Selects Collection**. This collection begins with
3 FREE books and 2 FREE gifts in the first shipment. Along with my 3 free books,
I'll also get 4 more books from the Harlequin Selects Collection, which I may either
return and owe nothing or keep for the low price of $24.14 U.S./$28.82 CAN. each
plus $2.99 U.S./$7.49 CAN. for shipping and handling per shipment*.If I decide to
continue, I will get 6 or 7 more books (about once a month for 7 months) but will only
need to pay for 4. That means 2 or 3 books in every shipment will be FREE! If I decide
to keep the entire collection, I'll have paid for only 32 books because 19 were FREE!
I understand that accepting the 3 free books and gifts places me under no obligation
to buy anything. I can always return a shipment and cancel at any time. My free
books and gifts are mine to keep no matter what I decide.

☐ 262 HCN 5576   ☐ 462 HCN 5576

Name (please print)

Address   Apt. #

City   State/Province   Zip/Postal Code

Mail to the Harlequin Reader Service:
IN U.S.A.: P.O. Box 1341, Buffalo, NY 14240-8531
IN CANADA: P.O. Box 603, Fort Erie, Ontario L2A 5X3

---

*Terms and prices subject to change without notice. Prices do not include sales taxes, which will be charged (if applicable) based
on your state or country of residence. Canadian residents will be charged applicable taxes. Offer not valid in Quebec. All orders
subject to approval. Credit or debit balances in a customer's account(s) may be offset by any other outstanding balance owed by
or to the customer. Please allow 3 to 4 weeks for delivery. Offer available while quantities last. © 2020 Harlequin Enterprises ULC.
® and ™ are trademarks owned by Harlequin Enterprises ULC.

Your Privacy—Your information is being collected by Harlequin Enterprises ULC, operating as Harlequin Reader Service. To see
how we collect and use this information visit https://corporate.harlequin.com/privacy-notice. From time to time we may also exchange
your personal information with reputable third parties. If you wish to opt out of this sharing of your personal information, please
visit www.readerservice.com/consumerschoice or call 1-800-873-8635. Notice to California Residents—Under California law, you
have specific rights to control and access your data. For more information visit https://corporate.harlequin.com/california-privacy.

50BOOKHS22R